THE PRODUCERS

START THE REVOLUTION WITHOUT ME

QUACKSER FORTUNE HAS A COUSIN IN THE BRONX

YOUNG FRANKENSTEIN

BLAZING SADDLES

THE ADVENTURES OF SHERLOCK HOLMES' SMARTER BROTHER

SILVER STREAK

That list reads like a *What's What in Great American Comedy* — and the common ingredient to all those films has been GENE WILDER. Now, in THE WORLD'S GREATEST LOVER, the actor-writer-director-producer has created one of the wildest, zaniest, most hilarious comedies ever to come to the screen. And who else but the brilliant Gene Wilder could rival the legendary sex symbol, Rudolph Valentino!

THE WORLD'S GREATEST LOVER and GENE WILDER — a combination that is unbeatable in American film comedy.

THE PLAYERS

Rudy .... Gene Wilder
Annie .... Carol Kane
Zitz .... Dom DeLuise
Hotel Manager .... Fritz Feld
Uncle Harry .... Carl Ballantine
Valentino .... Matt Collins
Tony Lassiter .... Richard Dimitri
Cousin Buddy .... Buddy Silberman
Barber .... Michael Huddleston
Mr. Kipper .... Lou Cutell
The Boss .... Michael Huddleston's Father
Bakery Foreman .... Charles Knapp
Anne Calassandro .... Candice Azzara

Written and Directed by
Gene Wilder

The World's Greatest Lover

Novelization by Chris Greenbury
Based on a screenplay by Gene Wilder

ace books

A Division of Charter Communications Inc.
A GROSSET & DUNLAP COMPANY
1120 Avenue of the Americas
New York, New York 10036

THE WORLD'S GREATEST LOVER

An ACE Book

First Ace Printing: December 1977

Published simultaneously in Canada

Printed in U.S.A.

CHAPTER 1

VALENTINO'S EYES maintained their devastating glare, even though he was in obvious pain. A huge hand smashed across the movie star's face, bringing a trickle of blood to his lip. Chained to the wall, he still fixed his eyes to those of his captor, as a fist landed full in his stomach.

"*Ooofff!*" cried Annie, as if she had had the blow delivered to her own stomach. She threw herself forward on the movie theatre seat, showering popcorn onto the floor. It was only then that she realized people were looking at her and she slipped to the back of her seat, lowering her wide, blue eyes with embarrassment. It was 1926 and respectable women didn't go to the movies alone.

Valentino looked down at her from his silver screen and smiled sympathetically. She knew *he* understood.

Annie Hickman walked quickly through the wet streets of Milwaukee after the film. She didn't like walking alone at night, but there was no choice. She couldn't stay home every evening while Rudy worked his night shift. It would drive her crazy.

A quiet, simple girl who liked to escape to her own, private world, Annie was one of life's victims. Perhaps that's why she was married to Rudy. Two misfits in a world that seemed to be passing them by. They could huddle together, sheltering themselves from life's problems.

She relaxed her pace a little, imagining that Valentino was looking out for her on her path home.

"Don't ever do that again!"

Adolph Zitz, movie mogul and midget monster, had just received a large blob of shaving cream, which covered most of his face.

"No, sir, I was a little nervous," stammered the new barber. Zitz looked up at him menacingly and wiped the cream from his eye with his pinky. Despite the barber's bulk, there was fear in his soul.

"Gentlemen, I am not a child, and I don't wish to be treated as one. Is that understood?"

Seven identical executives formed a semicircle around the mogul's chair. In complete unison, they gave a resounding:

"Yes, sir!"

"Now here's the question: If you went up to any bum on the street and asked him which is the biggest studio in Hollywood . . . . . what would he say?"

Without even looking, Zitz's arm shot out, pointing to the first yes-man.

"Rainbow, home of the stars!" came the instant reply.

"All right now." The menacing finger traveled to the next man. "I don't want any of that baloney."

"I would say Wainbow . . . Wainbow Studios," replied the second yes-man. He could never pronounce his 'R's. "It's the wargest and best!"

"*Save it*, save that yes-man shit. You think I need this kind of babying?" Obviously irritated by the pat reply, Zitz pointed to the third yes-man, a Chinese man with a Swedish upbringing.

"Rainbow, Rainbow Studios. I don't think there's any question about dat. Ha-yah."

"For crying out loud, will you cut it out!" A tear rolled down the cheek of the little man and landed on the shaking hand of the barber, who was still trying to shave the cream-filled face. "I know you want me to feel better, but this isn't the way."

There was absolutely no question in the fourth man's voice.

"Rainbow, Rainbow Studios, home of the stars!"

Zitz's voice was breaking as he tried to swallow

the large lump in his throat. He became over-whelmed by the replies.

"Christ, have I failed so badly? All I want is the truth.Isn't there one honest man in the room?"

Zitz's finger moved along the line, this time stopping at the preoccupied barber, only because he happened to be next in line. The hand could have held a loaded gun, as the barber's face turned a sheepish white.

"Well . . . uh, well . . . . . Paramount, I guess."

All the yes-men lowered their heads as Zitz turned to look at the person who had given him the answer. His face had a soothing smile, as if some angelic calm had overcome him.

"That's interesting. Why would you say that?" Zitz asked.

"Well, they have Rudolph Valentino," the barber replied. At the mention of the Valentino's name, Zitz leaped out of his chair and grabbed the barber's neck.

"Son of a bitch asshole *bastard! You're a lying traitor, did ya know that?*" Zitz bent the barber back onto a crescent-shaped desk and started to strangle the astonished man, as the other men tried to restrain him.

"Did ya know that, you *dirty dog-do pisshead fart blossom?*"

Just as they managed to remove Zitz's hands from the barber's throat, he threw them all off with amazing strength.

"*All right* . . . Leave me alone, all right! I'm

okay. Maybe this was a good thing. Give me a little perspective."

Zitz straightened himself out and sat back in the barber's chair. The yes-men carried the frightened barber back to his starting position, as the Chinese executive comforted the mogul by whispering sympathetic Swedish in his ear.

"Vi tycker allaomdej, Mr. Zitz. Vi tycker allaomdej. Yah!"

"Don't get too close to the middle here," Zitz said, pointing to the split in his moustache. "I hate it when I get nicked in this little part here." The barber shook his petrified head and started to mix another bowl of shaving cream.

"Now, lemme think, lemme think, . . . *Aaaaaggghhhhh!*"

The mogul's yell of inspiration made the now petrified barber jerk the shaving cream into the air, most of it landing in his own face, but he carried on professionally.

"Now listen to me very carefully," said Zitz. "The women in this country are so sex-starved... they'll accept the first pretty face that comes along and make him a star. Well, what would they do if they heard that Rainbow Studios was going to find the *greatest lover in America?*"

Zitz's voice had taken on a strange, hypnotic quality. He had a captive audience.

"I'm talking about someone who will make Rudolph Valentino look like a part-time nurse."

"Wow!"

"You can say that again," said Zitz. "Now what I . . . . ." He paused and looked at his men threateningly.

"*Wow!*" they replied.

They were mesmerized by his power and enthusiasm.

"*All right!*" Zitz yelled.

The men started to scurry around the room, taking notes and picking up telephones. The barber picked up his razor and tried to shave the yelling face of the tiny tyrant, as he barked out his orders.

"Get me the press, get me the radio, get me the fashion magazines, get me the trade papers, get me the columnists. We'll get lovers from every big city and hick town on the map. Because, gentlemen . . . I promise that within two weeks every male in America between the ages of seventeen and fifty-five is going to stop for one moment and at least *think* about coming to Hollywood to screen test for the biggest chance of his life!"

He stood in his barber's chair and looked at all of his men triumphantly.

"The chance to star in the new Rainbow Studios' film, *The World's Greatest Lover* . . . Now how's that for an idea?"

Zitz pointed at each man, demanding a spontaneous reaction.

"Great!" cried the first yes-man.

"Gweat, Mr. Zitz," echoed the second.

"Oh, great, just great!" said the Chinese man.

"Great, great, great!" cried the fourth.

"Ve-ry good," said the barber. Then, realizing his mistake, he quickly threw away his razor.

"I mean *great!"*

Zitz tried to restrain himself, but his hands were already in the "kill" position. An uncontrollable urge forced him towards the barber's throat.

"Too late!"

CHAPTER 2

The Milwaukee Gazette
January 4, 1926

WHO WILL BE
"THE WORLD'S GREATEST LOVER"?

RUDY HICKMAN was a daydreamer. It wasn't just the *idea* of something happening that drove him on to further extremes. He was absolutely *convinced* that greatness lay ahead.

Although he'd had many hair-brained ideas in the past, this time it was different. He knew he had to go to Hollywood. It was a feeling he'd never had before. He became obsessed. Nothing would get in his way.

Especially not his ridiculous job at a Milwaukee bakery. Everything was automated. He was only there to make sure nothing went wrong. The machines passed out a monotonous line of whipped cream cakes, one after the other. He sat and supervised little cherries plopping onto each cake. It was like counting sheep.

The clatter of machines seemed far away, as Rudy drifted into a deep sleep. He pictured himself in front of the movie cameras and dreamed of sheiks and stardom. Adoring women lined his path, eager for his affections. His name in lights. Admiration and success.

Suddenly, everything went wrong.

Rudy woke up being dragged along with a row of cakes towards a perilous opening in a giant machine. Somehow he'd gotten his hand caught up in the rubber conveyor belt.

He grabbed desperately at levers as blobs of whipped cream 'plooped' into his ears. Rainbow-colored frosting poured onto his head, followed by silver sequins and a cherry, as he disappeared through the hole in the machine.

A frantic foreman screamed orders to bring the screeching monster to a halt. A hush fell over the factory. It was a mortal sin for anyone to stop the machine. Production targets wouldn't be met. Profit ratios would be ruined. What the hell had happened?

A cake box, neatly wrapped with a red bow, popped out of the machine, followed by the rest of Rudy's body.

The foreman turned purple as he screamed at Rudy's head through a crack in the cake box. Rudy felt something solid in his hand, as he reached up and tried to pull himself out of the machine. As he grasped blindly for a lever, a sticky sludge of syrup poured over the foreman's head.

Rudy sensed something had gone wrong.

Moments later, Rudy sat in the boss's office, his head hung very low. Behind him sat the foreman, still covered with syrup.

"You know I want to help you," said the boss, a kindly man who just wanted his life to go smoothly. "You're a very nice boy, Rudy. You're like a son to me . . . did you know that? My own son! But you've got to come to your senses. If you could just realize that you are a *nothing* . . . that you were born a nothing . . . that you'll always be a nothing. Then maybe you could be happy. Now doesn't that make sense?"

The boss's heartfelt sermon was dismissed by Rudy with a shrug. Frustrated, the boss turned to the foreman.

"He still doesn't believe it. *Your dreams are killing you, did you know that?*" he screamed at Rudy.

Now he grabbed Rudy by the collar and dragged him over to a mirror.

"Look in the mirror! I said *look*! . . . . . Is that the face of a movie star?"

Rudy stared into the mirror, looking long and hard at himself. Suddenly, he heard tango music playing in his head. He flared his eyes, as he had seen Valentino do in the movies.

"Get him out of here!"

10

CHAPTER 3

RUDY'S NEXT JOB was as a sales assistant in a pastry shop. Now he had to deal with people, as opposed to machines. It added to his frustrations. People changing their minds all the time. Having to smile. "Thank you" and "please." It was just too much for him. His nerves started to tell.

"Rudy . . . I'm told that when you're nervous, you stick your tongue out at people. Is that true?" his new boss asked patiently.

Rudy sat silent. There was just no point in answering a question as ridiculous as that. Kipper, the weasely manager of the shop, hovered nearby.

"Mr. Kipper says that when you're nervous you either stick your tongue out or else you get hysterical laryngitis. Now what do you say to that?"

Rudy's face broke into a smile. The whole thing really was absurd.

"I don't know what he's talking about."

"Fibber!" gasped Kipper.

"Stop it!" said the boss. "Now, Rudy . . . you were fired from your last job for daydreaming. I want to give you the benefit of the doubt, but you've only been with us for four days; Mr. Kipper has been my manager for nine years. Why would he lie?"

The boss was in a sticky situation. The whole thing did seem ridiculous, but how could he question the word of his trusted manager? He walked over to his desk and lit a cigar to calm his nerves.

"I don't know," stammered Rudy. "Maybe I get a little hoarse sometimes . . . you know, from talking with all the customers and trying to do my best . . . but I don't know what he means about sticking my tongue out. That's crazy. Why would I do a thing like that?"

Rudy stuck out his tongue.

"He did it," squealed Kipper.

"When?" said the boss, spinning around to look. Rudy had retracted his tongue.

"Just now. While you were lighting your cigar," said Kipper.

"Did you do it?" inquired the boss to Rudy.

"No."

"He's lying," yelled Kipper.

"Tell the truth, Rudy!" pleaded the boss.

"I don't know what he's talking about," said Rudy.

"Rudy, are you a little nervous?" asked the

boss. He turned his back to put a match in the ashtray on his desk.

"Not at all," croaked Rudy in a hoarse voice.

The boss whipped his head around and stared at Rudy full in the face.

"What?"

"I say, not at all," coughed Rudy, clearing his throat. The boss turned away again.

Rudy stuck out his tongue.

"He did it again!" Kipper yelled.

The boss's head whipped back and glared. "Did you do it?"

"No," Rudy said.

"Kipper?" the boss asked.

"Lying! lying! lying!" squealed Kipper.

"Rudy . . . the truth!" the boss demanded.

"I did not do that," Rudy said firmly.

The boss turned and reached for a glass of water on his desk. Things had become frantic.

"Why would I do a thing like that?" said Rudy. "Do you think I'm crazy?"

"*Yaaaagh!*" Kipper dived for Rudy's tongue as it popped out again.

"What happened . . . did he do it?" asked the bewildered boss.

"Give it back to me, you cheater," shouted Kipper frantically.

The boss pushed Kipper out of the way and grabbed Rudy by the shoulder.

"Rudy . . . . . for the last time . . . . . did you do it?"

Rudy covered his face with his hands and shook his head. The boss squeezed and pulled and finally managed to pry Rudy's hands open.

His tongue was sticking four inches out of his mouth.

"*You're fired!*"

CHAPTER 4

ANNIE SAT IN HER nightgown at the dressing table. As she gently brushed her hair, she could see Rudy in the reflection of the mirror, sulking.

"Rudy, you *do* stick out your tongue. Or sometimes, you get laryngitis, just for a moment. But it won't last. Those are just little nervous habits, because you're so high-strung. You mustn't think about them. Even the third thing . . . " She stopped in mid-sentence and bit her lip.

Rudy raised his head. "What?" he asked.

"I said . . . even the third thing . . . oh, it's nothing."

Annie tried to dismiss it. This wasn't the time to add to Rudy's misery.

"What third thing?" Rudy's face started to change color as he felt his blood racing.

"Well . . . when you get angry, you . . . oh, it's not even worth talking about," said Annie.

Rudy walked over to Annie and snatched the

hairbrush from her, demanding an answer.

"What third thing?"

"Well, sometimes, when you get angry . . . you twist your words around so that they don't make sense," she said cautiously.

Rudy became hot under the collar.

"I do not twist my words around," he said indignantly.

"But you do, darling."

Rudy turned red.

"I do not do that!"

"Rudy . . . I've seen it happen. I couldn't make up a thing like that. You know I would never want to hurt your feelings . . ."

"Are you trying to give me fart hailure?" he yelled angrily. Then he paused and thought for a second. No, that was what he had meant to say.

"Well, maybe I was mistaken about the third thing. I'm sorry," said Annie.

As always, she tried to recover. If she didn't soften the blow, no one else would.

Rudy buried his head in his pillow. "I'm going crazy in Milwaukee! I don't want to be Rudy Hickman. I'm selling the house; I'm selling the car; I'm changing my name. We're going to Hollywood!"

"Hollywood?" Annie was stunned. The image of Rudolph Valentino flashed through her mind.

"I've got to try out for that contest. My Uncle Harry knows people out there. He'll help us," he said.

Annie had to be very careful. Rudy's ego was already bruised. But this time, she had every right to object. Her whole life was being threatened. It wouldn't just set them back like Rudy's other schemes. This might ruin them.

"There'll be thousands of men, Rudy," she said.

"I can win it!"

"They'll be coming from all over America."

"I can win it!" he yelled.

"Rudy, they'll be professionals."

He'd made up his mind. For years, people had laughed at him. All the years of frustration had taken their toll.

"*I said I can win it. Now light the bed to out come turn on!*"

Annie couldn't sleep that night. Her mind was racing, filled with anxiety, as she lay wide-eyed awake. It didn't help that Rudy was snoring in her ear. How could she handle the dilemma she was in? Fate, without Annie having consciously exerted an ounce of will, was suddenly going to bring her close to the only person who really understood her.

She slipped quietly out of bed and crossed the floor to the dresser. Hidden between two sweaters in the bottom drawer was a buff-colored envelope. Tiptoeing over to the window, she pulled out a photograph and held it up to the moonlight. The inscription on the photo read:

To Annie,

    You seem sensitive. If you're ever in Hollywood . . .

                           Rudolph Valentino

Annie sat gazing out at the rooftops of Milwaukee. Her thoughts were far away. She bunched her knees up under her chin, like a child, and cradled the photograph of Valentino in her arms. For the first time that night, she closed her eyes, as a soothing drowziness overcame her. As sleep took her, she smiled softly.

CHAPTER 5

THE NEXT FEW DAYS were tragic. Annie watched all the things that she and Rudy possessed disappear in a frantic effort to scrape some money together. Probably the worst part was the smirking and laughter that went on behind Rudy's back as he virtually gave things away for the cause. The humiliation was unbearable, but Rudy went about his task with a strength that Annie had never seen before. He was absolutely determined to make this chance work. He dedicated a lot of time to finding a new wardrobe. With the change in his character, he had also adopted a new physical appearance and many people seemed mildly impressed by his new image. It was then that Rudy Hickman changed his name to Rudy Valentine.

The crowded railway coach and the long journey from Milwaukee to Chicago to Los Angeles took its toll on both of them. Annie was exhausted and confused by all the things that had happened in such a short time.

She huddled close to Rudy and slept, wrapped in an American Railways blanket to keep warm. Rudy dozed, as he cradled Annie in his arms. His mind again traveled to movie sets.

"Los Angeles next."

Rudy opened his eyes and realized where he was. He opened a travel bag that was resting on his lap and took out a small face mirror. He looked at his face and pinched his cheeks for color, then placed the mirror back in the case and laid it down by his side. On the lid, in large letters, his suitcase read: RUDY VALENTINE.

Just then the car was plunged into darkness as the train went into a long tunnel. The train lurched violently a couple of times in the dark.

As it came back into the light, Rudy could see that it hadn't affected anyone. They were all still fast asleep.

He leaned over and spoke sweetly into the blanket that Annie was wrapped in.

"Is this my little poopie?"

The blanket stirred a little.

"Poopie, poopie, poopie, poopie. Good morning, my little bride. It's time to get up. Time for yum yums."

He whistled romantically into her ear.

From out of the blanket emerged the head of a small, bald man. Somehow, during the lurching in the tunnel, everybody had been thrown into a different place and the little chap had ended up in between Rudy and Annie. He glared at Rudy very suspiciously and then changed his seat.

Rudy moved across the seat and again tried to wake Annie as gently as he could.

"Darling," Rudy hummed softly.

Annie woke with a start, screaming as she sat bolt upright:

"I said 'No!' You filthy pig!"

Rudy quickly glanced at all the people in the coach car, who were staring at him. He flushed with embarrassment.

Annie, now fully awake, started to rub the sleep out of her eyes.

"What? Oh! Good morning, darling. Are we almost there?"

Rudy forced a smile and nodded. Annie got up and gave Rudy a quick kiss on the cheek.

"I'll just go and splash some water on my face," Annie said, as she walked towards the ladies' toilet at the end of the car.

Rudy watched her go. He gazed around the carriage at the other passengers. On the opposite seat sat an attractive young girl, who caught sight of Rudy at exactly the same time.

They stared for a moment, then Rudy tried out a "Valentino look" on her, flaring his eyes and looking deep and hard at her.

The girl smiled. She was obviously attracted to him.

Rudy was a little surprised. He looked away for

a moment, hiding a smile. Then he quickly turned his head back and flared his eyes again. This time, his eyes were crossed.

The girl burst into laughter, then looked back to see what Rudy would do next.

Rudy began to try another "look" on her, but stopped when he noticed a large man walking down the corridor towards the girl. Her reaction immediately changed as the man stood by her. She started to kiss his hand as he glared at Rudy menacingly.

Rudy put his arms around the blanketed body next to him and kissed its head, again thinking that it was Annie. He smiled sheepishly at the scowling boyfriend and began to nibble the ear of . . . the bald man again!

The mortified man pulled back the blanket and stared at him with disgust. Rudy sank back into his seat and stared out of the window.

Suddenly, a beautiful young girl appeared outside his window. She had love in her eyes as she ran alongside the train, staring at Rudy with desire.

Rudy thought there must be some mistake. He looked behind him, but there was no one. He looked back out the window. The girl had been joined by another, equally beautiful, girl and they were waving at him. Soon there were five, then eight, then sixteen girls . . . all following Rudy's window with tears in their eyes, hankies in their hands. They threw kisses and reached out for him.

Rudy was overcome. His eyes filled with tears as he became overwhelmed with emotion. He struggled to open the window. With great effort, he finally flung the window up and reached out to the girls.

"Yes! Yes! I'm here! How did you know? I don't understand . . . I just decided to come three days ago . . . ."

"Cut! Cut! Cut!"

Immediately, the girls' attitude changed. They stopped running and walked over to a small film crew, who were filming the farewell scene from their movie. A frantic director screamed at Rudy through a bullhorn.

"I knew some idiot would spoil my farewell. I knew some stupid putz would spoil my farewell." The director turned to his assistant, who was standing next to him, and yelled through the horn.

"When's the next train?"

"Twenty-five minutes," the assistant replied.

"All right, break them, break them."

"But the light is changing."

"Who gives a shit!" roared the director through the horn.

A bewildered Rudy pulled his head back inside the train and started to take down a bag from the overhanging rack.

"Los Angeles, California," cried the conductor. "Home of the stars . . . and lots of featured players. Los Angeles next, Los Angeles!"

The California sun shone through Rudy's coach car window as the train started to slow down for the last time after its long journey.

Rudy removed his overcoat, revealing a beautiful white genuine imitation Valentino suit. He took down a stylish Valentino hat from an overhanging rack and placed it on his head, checking his reflection in the train window. A line of people started to move towards the exit as Annie reappeared. Suddenly, a wave of terror flooded over her and she panicked.

"I'm plain! I'm a plain, simple girl! I've never left Milwaukee in my life! Uncle Harry will hate me! Rudy—what am I going to do?"

"Now stop it," said Rudy. "I have enough on my mind without having to deal with this childishness. If you're going to get hysterical, I won't even let you off the train. Now calm down and stop acting like a baby."

Rudy's harsh reply seemed to pull Annie together and she became a little embarrassed by her outburst.

"I'm sorry. I won't do it again," she said. "What time is your screen test tomorrow?"

"Twelve thirty." Rudy's eyes popped. He had suddenly contracted his hysterical laryngitis.

"What?" said Annie.

"Twelve thirty," croaked Rudy again. "Oh, shit!" Rudy cleared his throat and tried to speak normally, but his words still came out in a raspy whisper.

"We shouldn't mention that word any more," said Annie.

"What word?" asked Rudy in a suddenly normal voice.

"Screen test."

"Why not?" croaked Rudy, once again in his whisper.

"We'd better drop the subject," said Annie.

"Don't can I what I say and say can't tell me!" roared Rudy.

"I'm sorry," said Annie.

"Didn't you say you wanted me to try?" Rudy asked.

"I do want you to try. But I didn't know you had your heart set on winning."

"Did you think I wanted to come in *thirteenth?*" screamed Rudy.

"But what happens if you don't win the screen test?" asked Annie.

"I *will* win!" croaked Rudy as the laryngitis reappeared.

They were approaching the door of the train. Rudy became determined to beat his affliction.

"Screen test, screen test, screen test." He tried to strangle the words out.

"Screen test, screen test . . . " he said in a half voice.

"Screen test! I will win that screen test!" Rudy's voice finally rang out loud and clear. Perhaps a

little too loud because it made everybody in the coach car turn and stare at him. Rudy was oblivious.

"Not because I'm the most handsome man in the world," he went on. "Not because I'm the sexiest man in the world. Not because I'm the best actor in the world . . . " Rudy stepped down from the train and onto the station platform.

"But because *I am unique!"*

He turned around to find himself surrounded by a sea of men, all dressed in genuine imitation Valentino suits with belted backs, just like his. Rudy's mouth fell open. He grabbed their suitcases and plowed through the throng of men. Annie tried to keep up with Rudy's furious pace, but she was hampered by the fact that she kept grabbing the wrong man's arm.

"Sorry! Oh, excuse me—I thought you were someone else," she continually exclaimed to each Rudy she thought she had finally caught.

CHAPTER 6

THE MOVIE SCREEN flickered into life in the dark screening room. Executives surrounded Adolph Zitz, who was lying on a portable table, wrapped in a white sheet. The barber was doing his best to massage the movie mogul in the semidarkness.

On the screen, an actor, dressed as a sheik, rode brilliantly at a canter towards the camera. As the horse reached its mark, it came to a dead halt. The actor sailed through the air, landing head first in a pile of sand.

Zitz stared at the screen without blinking. The yes-men sitting around him lowered their eyes.

"When's the final audition?" Zitz asked.

"Friday, Mr. Zitz," came the reply.

"How many 'rottens' have we got?"

A yes-man looked at his pad. "Twenty-three hundred."

Zitz put his head in his hands. "How many 'fairly rottens'?"

"Fourteen," said the yes-man.

"Have we got a 'doesn't stink'?"

"No, sir."

"We don't have one 'doesn't stink'?"

"Not yet, sir."

The second screen test started. Another actor stopped his horse brilliantly, dismounted and, with great bravado, took the leading lady into his arms. He spoke passionately to her, their lips almost touching.

He had terrible breath.

The leading lady turned her head and blew his breath away, then she valiantly tried to carry on.

The actor continued smiling as he spoke passionately into her nose. She had to turn away again. She spoke to somebody on the set and the screen test director came into the shot and started to talk to the actor. The actor spoke into the director's face.

The director fainted.

As assistants rushed in to help, the actor turned to the camera and shrugged his shoulders.

"Out of eleven thousand men to pick from, all I want is three finalists and I can't find one 'doesn't stink'!" Zitz yelled.

"Look, Mr. Zitz!"

A third screen test had started and a very good-looking actor rode up and went through his actions perfectly.

"Who's that?" asked Zitz.

"His name is Robert Drake."

"Not bad, not too bad." Zitz was getting a little excited. "Look at him. Look, look. I think he's got something."

They all stared at the screen, eager to see his next move.

Zitz motioned his head towards each man. "Whaddya think?" he asked.

"Not too bad, not too bad," said the first yes-man.

"He's not too bad, Mr. Zitz," replied the second man.

"Yah! I really think he's not too bad," said the third.

"Not too bad at all, really . . . not bad," said the fourth.

Zitz motioned to the barber, who tried to politely pass his turn on. He still had band-aids on his face from their last encounter.

"No, you! You! What did you think?" demanded Zitz to the barber.

"Oh . . . I . . . . . ohh," stammered the barber.

"Say it!" said Zitz.

"Well, uh . . . well . . . I think there's something strange about that fellow."

They all turned and looked back at the movie screen.

Robert Drake, filled with emotion, suddenly lifted his head from the leading lady's shoulder and turned his head to face full into the camera.

His eyes were crossed to the point of no return. "*Yaaaghhh!*" screamed Zitz as he sandwiched the barber in the middle of the collapsed massage table and tried to crush him to death. The yes-men just watched dejectedly as the lights came up.

"Always right, aren't you? Gotta always be right!" yelled Zitz, trying to crush the barber between the two halves of the portable massage table.

During the confusion and shouting, a projectionist poked his head out from the projection booth to see what was going on.

"Whadidya think of today's stuff, Mr. Adolph?" he asked.

Zitz froze. He climbed off the table-and-barber sandwich he had made and started to twitch. All heads turned to the projectionist in astonishment. Zitz's tongue seemed tied to the bottom of his mouth.

"You dumb schmuck!" he exploded. But the projectionist seemed oblivious to any anger coming his way. He continued his conversation with Zitz as if they were old friends.

"No good, huh? You wanna hear what they did at Paramount?"

"Waaaghh?" gargled Zitz.

"When they used to have their big auditions, they gave out thousands of phonograph records with a director telling the actors exactly what to do. Great idea, huh? That's why they're tops, Zitzie."

Zitz calmly walked over to two of his yes-men and cracked their heads together.

"That idea *stiiinks!*"

"Sure beats the shit we've seen today," replied the projectionist nonchalantly.

That was enough for Zitz. His face started to turn colors and his hands began to tremble. It seemed as if he couldn't breathe. His uncontrollable urge to demolish overcame him once again and he went for the man's throat.

"I'm in the union, Mr. Zitz."

Zitz froze. He didn't know what to do with his hands, which were suspended in midair, the fingers aching to kill someone. Suddenly, he grabbed his own throat and smashed his head so far into the wall that it disappeared.

"By the way," the projectionist seemed more casual than ever, "that's how they found Rudolph Valentino."

From inside the wall came a small tremor.

"*Get me that record!*" Zitz's voice boomed out, sending the yes-men into a flurry. They grabbed for telephones and notebooks as the voice from the wall gave them their orders.

"I want two thousand records delivered within the next twenty-four hours, and I'm not just whistling Dixie!"

The barber, who had been spared any further torture by the unexpected intrusion of the projectionist, stood in a corner of the room, singing to himself.

"You wanna sign for the room, Mr. Zitz?" The projectionist handed the body a receipt book and pen. Zitz searched for the pen with his hand and signed the book, with the projectionist guiding him.

"What kind of a record, Mr. Zitz?" asked one of his yes-men.

"Round, a round one!" came the pained reply, still from inside the wall. "Just like Paramount's. Oh, Jesus, why do I have to think of everything? It's too lonely up here. Do I have to come up with every single goddamn thing myself? Use your heads, for Christ's sake! What am I paying you guys for?"

The barber continued humming quietly in the corner. His eyes seemed happier now, and he even smiled as he occasionally sucked his thumb.

CHAPTER 7

HOLLYWOOD! RUDY AND ANNIE sat in the back of the taxicab, awestruck, as they gazed at the palatial homes and the streets lined with giant palm trees. Neither spoke to each other. Milwaukee seemed far away now.

Music suddenly blared out behind them. As they turned to look, a Rainbow Studios van started to overtake them. On the side of the van was a huge sign:

WHO WILL BE THE
WORLD'S GREATEST LOVER?

The Poinsettia was considered to be the most fashionable hotel in Los Angeles, especially for those members of the film industry who planned their visits there carefully, so that they might be seen in the Poinsettia Bar or the dining room or the Garden Terrace, laughing and dancing, unconscious of the outside world that was watching them.

Rudy and Annie entered the giant lobby, with its high ceilings and ornate furniture. Walking through such a sea of opulence made them suddenly realize how insignificant they really were.

"Paging Mr. Rudy Valentine. Mr. Valentine, please. Paging Mr. Rudy Valentine!"

They looked at each other in bewilderment. From the other side of the lobby, a fancily dressed chauffeur was paging Rudy. Of course, it was Cousin Buddy! Rudy's face lit up with excitement, but then he quickly checked himself and tried to put on a dignified air. Cousin Buddy was up to something; he always had a scheme.

"I am Mr. Valentine," said Rudy, keeping a formal distance from his childhood playmate.

"*You* are Mr. Rudy Valentine?" asked Buddy, so loudly that three or four guests turned their heads.

"Yes," said Rudy. Then, under his breath, he said to Buddy, "Not so much!"

"Oh! So you are Mr. *Rudy Valentine!*" replied Buddy, even louder. His words echoed around the lobby.

"Yes! Not so much, not so much," Rudy urged in a hoarse whisper. "This is Annie. This is my cousin, Buddy."

"Hi," said Buddy under his breath.

"Hello," said Annie shyly.

"Where's Uncle Harry?" asked Rudy.

"He's getting you a phonograph record to practice with," Buddy whispered. "Oh, by the way," he suddenly shouted again, *"The studio will be sending a great big car to pick you up tomorrow."*

"Thank you," Rudy replied formally.

"Oh, that's all right, Mr. Valentine." Buddy grabbed Rudy's hand and started to shake it. "You're going to be a very famous movie star in a few weeks," he said.

The whole scene did not go unnoticed. The hotel manager was now watching with great interest.

"A twenty-dollar bill. Wow! What a big tip!" hollered Buddy. His playacting was going a little too far now.

"Get the hell out of here," Rudy whispered.

As quickly as he had appeared, Buddy left. As he made his final exit, he shouted, *"Oh boy! A twenty-dollar tip from a famous movie star!"*

Buddy's performance had made quite an effect. Heads followed with interest as Rudy and Annie walked towards the registrar's desk. As they approached the desk, the hotel manager came out to greet them. Rudy nervously tried to introduce himself.

"How do you do? I am Mr . . . ."

"Oh, my!" interrupted the manager.

Rudy and Annie looked at each other. Rudy tried again to introduce himself.

"Uh. I am Mr . . . . "

"Oh, My!"

"Yes, and this is my wife, Mrs. . . . "

"Oh, my!" The manager seemed to be in rapture. Rudy just seemed confused.

"Good!" said Rudy. "Well, I believe there is a room under the name of . . . "

"Rudy Valentine," interrupted the manager again. Buddy's performance had been most effective.

"How nice of you to know," said Rudy.

"Please." The manager excused himself and snapped his fingers to a room clerk. "Mr. Valentine's key, please. Room 203."

"He's in 814," replied the clerk.

Like a bolt of lightning, the manager's hand shot out and slapped the clerk across the face.

"203, please," he smiled, and the clerk responded immediately. "Right this way, Mr. Valentine." The manager snapped his fingers again. A porter followed with their suitcases.

"Second floor," he told the elevator attendant. Then, out of the corner of his eye, he noticed that Rudy's tongue was sticking out. He gave a polite smile and a little laugh as the elevator doors closed.

If the hotel lobby had seemed opulent, room 203 was a king's private sitting room. They descended three steps into the sunken living room. Across the room, there were steps leading to a sumptuous bed.

"Voilà!" exclaimed the manager. He looked at the room with affection and pride.

"Oh, Rudy," Annie gasped in awe.

"The sunken living room is a special feature of the Poinsettia," said the manager.

"It's very nice," Annie said.

The manager walked across the bedroom and pulled the drapes open to reveal French windows and a small balcony. The bed was a large four-poster with curtains all around it.

"We have only four rooms like it, but yours overlooks the Garden Terrace of our beautiful dining room just below."

The manager snapped his fingers again and a waiter appeared with a bucket of champagne.

"A little champagne . . . for madame."

"Oh, that's not . . . " Annie began, but she was interrupted by the manager's running speech.

"If there's anything you wish—day or night—please call," he said. "And now . . . " he snapped his fingers, "I leave you!"

The waiter and the porter disappeared.

"A tout à l'heure," the manager said, as he bowed.

"We will, thank you," said Annie.

And now they were alone. Music drifted up from the terrace below. Rudy walked to the French windows and stepped out onto the small balcony.

"Rudy . . . how can we afford all this?"

"Don't talk about money," said Rudy in a half voice.

"But Rudy . . . we only have . . . "

"Don't talk about money! My soul is on fire!"

Annie joined him out on the balcony. They looked down at the Garden Terrace. Couples danced to a small three-piece orchestra. The sun was going down, silhouetting the palm trees in the orange sky. A light breeze blew through Annie's hair. Rudy and Annie looked at each other.

"Do you hear that music?" he asked.

"Yes."

"Do you see that bed?" he asked.

"Yes."

"Does anything in particular come to mind?"

Annie paused for a moment.

"Yes," she said, with a slight blush.

"Shall we say . . . in twenty seconds?" said Rudy.

As Annie obediently started to prepare herself, Rudy grabbed her hand and pulled her back. He kissed her hand, as Valentino would have done. Then he let her go back into the bedroom.

Rudy stood out on the terrace, looking at the hills. "Hollywood!" he exclaimed to himself.

"What, darling?" Annie asked from the four-poster bed.

"Do you know what this means to me? These are my dreams. I'm looking at my dreams. Lillian Gish is in those hills. Douglas Fairbanks comes to this hotel for lunch."

He looked down at the couples dancing in the patio below.

"Famous people are dancing right below us . . . in the afternoon. Annie . . . one of those ladies dancing could be Greta Gar—"

Suddenly, his eyes fixed on her. The greatest screen goddess of all time was dancing just below him.

"*Aaah . . . aaah*. Ooh, Oooh!" She was actually there. It wasn't a dream. He could only make strange little noises.

"What did you say, darling?" asked Annie, from inside the bed.

"Oooh! Ooh! Ooh!" cooed Rudy.

"I won't be a minute," said Annie, slipping into her nightgown.

"Oowa wa wa. Wa wa wa!"

"Me, too, darling. Me, too." Annie smiled as she listened to his little cries.

"Oowa wa wa, wa, wa wa!"

Annie slipped into her nightdress and, like a child, enthusiastically burst through the drapes surrounding the bed.

"*Ready!*"

Rudy was in such a daze that when Annie popped out from behind the drapes, it knocked him off his balance. He fell backwards, over the balcony, and landed on the shoulders of the large man who was dancing with Greta Garbo. The big fellow broke Rudy's fall so effectively that Rudy just replaced him as Garbo's partner. He stared at her. Her fine, delicate features were covered with

a thin veil from her hat, but her beauty was inde-
scribable. Rudy finally plucked up the courage to
speak.

"Excuse me . . . are you really Greta?"

"No, my name is Ludwig," came the reply in a
deep German accent. It was a man!

"A lot of people say I look like her."

Rudy flushed red, but he was too embarrassed
to walk away. They continued dancing.

"Do you come here often?" asked Ludwig.

"No. This is my first time," said Rudy.

"Oh, good," the man in the dress began to hum
a tune in Rudy's ear. "It's very romantic here,
don't you think?"

"Yes, Ludwig," replied Rudy, flushing even
redder.

"Will I see you later?" asked Ludwig.

"I have to go home now." Rudy stopped dancing and walked away, trying not to move a mus-
cle.

Ludwig put his hands on his hips as he watched
Rudy leave.

"I always fall for the wrong guys," he said.

CHAPTER 8

RUDY AND ANNIE SAT in the magnificent dining room of the Poinsettia Hotel that evening. In the Garden terrace, just off the dining room, couples danced to a small combo. Others sat at candlelit tables, waiting for the next dance.

"You know," said Rudy, "if a man reaches his climax too soon . . . that's not necessarily a bad thing."

Annie just stared at him.

"That's right," he said. "It happens a lot with very passionate men."

"I don't know much about those things, Rudy. You're the only man I've ever been with."

A tango began to play.

"Did you know that our bed is right above this table?" asked Rudy softly.

They both looked up.

"No," said Annie.

"What number are we up to?"

"We just finished seven."

"I'd like to try number eight."

Rudy called to a nearby waiter. As he took out his wallet to pay the check, Annie's eyes widened as she contemplated "number eight."

Music from the Garden Terrace drifted up into the bedroom as Rudy and Annie climbed into the large, draped, four-poster bed. A book lay by the side of the bed, and on its cover, in large letters, it read:

SEX
BY THE NUMBERS
(THE ULTIMATE IN ECSTASY)

"Start number three," said Rudy, from inside the bed. "Good. That's good. All right, more number three, more number three, and . . . number *four!* Annie, don't stop three, just add number four!"

"I'm sorry," said Annie.

"Don't ever stop three! Three goes on all the time."

"Oh, I didn't realize that," she said.

"And three and four and four and three and give me a little five. Not too much, not too much! Good. All right, now listen to me, honey. I want you to start number seven!"

"Seven?" asked Annie.

"Don't argue! Just go right into seven. Number five . . . and *seven!* Number five and *seven!* Annie, you're stopping in the middle!"

"What about six?"

"*I'll do six.* Don't talk about six. Just go from five directly into seven. Do you understand?"

"All right, I'll try."

"That's a girl. That's it. Five…Seven! Five…seven! Get ready, we're going to try for number eight."

"Number eight?" echoed Annie, with fear and wonder in her voice.

"Don't get nervous. Just pretend it's like any other night. All right: when I say 'Go' . . . do exactly what the Indian lady does on page fourteen."

"Oh, you're kidding."

"Annie, . . . there's nothing to be afraid of. Just don't lose your concentration. Get ready now. More seven, more seven, more seven, and . . . *Now!* Good! Yes! That's it. That's it."

"Are we doing number eight?"

"Close! You're very close. Now take off your shoes and socks."

"How do I do that?"

"Annie, don't argue! Just do it!"

"Can I stop number three for a second?".

"You never stop three. Three goes on all the time. I told you that."

"But what happened to six?"

"*To hell with six! Will you forget six?*"

"Oh, Rudy."

"You're wonderful! I promise you can do it.

You've just got to have confidence."

"Is this it?"

"I love you, Annie."

"Is this it?"

"I love you, I love you, Annie."

"Are we doing number eight?"

"*Yes!* This is *Ei - yeah - yeah - yeah - yeahhht!*"

Loud snores could be heard coming from inside the four-poster later that night. After a few moments, Annie came out from behind the canopy, wearing her nightgown.

She got up and put on her robe, which was draped over a nearby chair. As she tied her robe, she walked to the balcony, looking back once to hear if Rudy was still sleeping. He still snored, but lighter now.

She gazed out over the balcony, at the couples dancing below. The band played a romantic melody as the couples clung to each other lovingly.

Annie turned back into the room and crept over to her suitcase, watching the four-poster for the slightest stir. She pulled out her autographed photo of Rudolph Valentino and read the inscription again:

"If ever you're in Hollywood . . .?"

Annie looked at the great lover's eyes, his mouth. She glanced back towards the bed once more. Then, still holding the picture, she started to think.

She silently slipped over to the bureau and started to write.

CHAPTER 9

"BUENOS DÍAS."

Dawn's first light shone through the bedroom, bathing it in a warm, yellow softness. A fresh scent filled the air.

Two gardeners in the courtyard below could be heard talking in Spanish as they cleared the tables to one side in order to water down the Garden Terrace.

Annie lifted her head suddenly. She had fallen asleep at the desk, across the room from the bed. She looked around quickly, but Rudy was snoring solidly inside the four-poster. On the desk lay the letter she had written the night before.

She read it again.

Dear Rudy,

We've been married for three months, and I feel as if I'm dying. My life has gone somewhere without me.

Rudolph Valentino has asked me to join

him. I think he is the only one who under-
stands me.

Please forgive me, Rudy, I can't live by
the numbers.

Love,
Annie

Annie addressed an envelope and put the letter
inside. Picking up her small suitcase, which was
already packed, she dropped the envelope on the
desk. She walked into the bathroom with her
things. Looking one more time towards the bed,
she closed the door gently. Then she turned on
the hot and cold bathtub faucets full force. With
the sound of water as her cover, she quickly
dressed.

Rudy stirred. He opened one eye and looked
around. He heard the water running, blinked two
or three times, and went back to sleep.

Annie patted her face with a cold washcloth,
then threw it towards the bathtub.

She opened the bathroom window, which led to
the fire escape, looked at herself quickly in the
mirror to adjust her hat, and then climbed through
the window, pulling her suitcase behind her.
What she didn't see was that the washcloth she
had thrown aside a moment before had knocked
the rubber bathtub stopper directly into the drain.
Water was filling the tub very rapidly.

Uncle Harry, Aunt Tillie, Cousin Corinne and

Cousin Max marched through the lobby of the Poinsettia Hotel like a procession of ducks. Uncle Harry led the way to the registrar's counter and addressed himself to the clerk.

"Who's in charge here?"

"Tomasso Aboloni," the nervous clerk replied. "He's the hotel manager."

"Where is he?"

"Right over there, sir."

Uncle Harry started away, then stopped to address the clerk again.

"Who do I ask for?"

"Aboloni!"

"A baloney?" Uncle Harry queried to himself. Well, it sounded a little crazy, but if those were the rules . . .

Uncle Harry walked up to the hotel manager, who was standing a few yards away. The manager was too busy writing in his registrar's book to notice Uncle Harry standing in front of him.

"I'd like a baloney," announced Uncle Harry.

The hotel manager looked up sharply.

"Yes, sir . . . right here."

"Where?" asked Uncle Harry.

The hotel manager pointed to himself.

"Here!" he said.

"So where's a baloney?" demanded Uncle Harry again.

"I'm Aboloni," said the manager.

"You're a baloney?" said Uncle Harry.

"That's right," said the manager.

Uncle Harry nodded. He had handled this type before.

"Once upon a time there were three bears," he began.

The hotel manager wasn't sure what he had just heard. "Pardon me?" he said.

"What did you do?" asked Uncle Harry.

"When?" asked the hotel manager.

"How do I know?" replied Uncle Harry.

"How do you know what?" the manager demanded.

"By practicing!" Uncle Harry shouted. "Constantly!"

"Practicing what?" the manager shouted back.

"Whatever you want!" Uncle Harry tried to explain. "I can't live your life for you."

"*Sir,*" exclaimed the manager, trying to regain his composure, "may we start again *please!*"

Uncle Harry was delighted. "You mean the three bears?"

"*What* three bears?" said the baffled manager.

"*Any* three bears!" said Harry. "What difference does it make? Do you have a thing about bears?"

"What is it that we are talking about?" asked the manager.

"Give me a hint," said Harry.

"Who are you, sir?" demanded the manager.

"I'm fine! Now will you please tell Mr. Rudy Valentine that Uncle Harry is downstairs, waiting."

"And you are, sir?"

"No, I'm Uncle Harry."

"Ah! It's you."

"Gesundheit!" said Harry, then turning to Aunt Tillie, he explained, "This guy could drive you nuts."

"*Listen to me!*" he yelled at the manager, "Just tell him that his Aunt Tillie and Uncle Harry are here."

The confused manager picked up the telephone and dialed.

The sound of the telephone ringing in Rudy's room was mixed with the sound of rushing water.

Rudy jumped up on the first ring, but he wasn't quite awake yet. He pulled the canopy open and made for the phone, which was on a small table in the sunken living room. Champagne bottle, bucket, silver tray and glasses floated by Rudy as he started down the steps. Suddenly, Rudy was wading up to his thighs in water. His eyes popped, as the phone continued to ring. Filled with confusion, he reached for the telephone that was floating by him.

"Hello?" he said.

"Aunt Tillie and Uncle Harry are here!" came the voice from the receiver.

"Aughh!" squealed Rudy.

"I'll send them right up," said the manager, as he hung up. "I think he was tickled pink," he said to Uncle Harry. "It's room 203. The elevator is just over there."

"Do you like shoes?" Harry asked the manager, with a suspicious look in his eyes.

"Yes," the manager answered haltingly.

"Wing tips? I mean . . . really pointy?" said Harry.

"Well . . . "

"All right, all right! Not in front of my family," Harry exclaimed. "Come on!"

The family started for the elevator as the hotel manager tried to figure out what had just been said.

A bewildered Rudy put down the phone. He waded towards the bathroom.

"Annie," he called out.

He reached the bathroom door and, as he opened it, a flood of water poured out. Rudy looked inside. No Annie. He quickly turned off the bathtub faucets. Then, picking up Annie's nightgown and robe from a little stool, he went back into the bedroom.

"Annie," he called out in panic.

Rudy froze. His eyes fixed on the envelope and he rushed to it, dropping Annie's robe, but still carrying her nightgown. He opened the envelope and read the letter. His eyes fixed on the words:

Rudolph Valentino has asked me to join him!

Rudy looked up. He was lost. He looked at Annie's nightgown, cradled in his arms as if he were carrying her, and sank to his knees.

There was a knock at the door. Rudy was almost catatonic. Half his body was immersed in the water.

"Come in!" he said, rising to his feet.

"Guess who's here?" said Harry as the family burst into the room.

They all stared at Rudy, holding Annie's nightgown full-length. Rudy's eyes were glazed.

"Hello, Uncle Harry. Hello, Aunt Tillie. Hi, Reenie. Hi, Max. Come in, won't you?"

But they couldn't come in too far without stepping into the water.

"Heh, heh, heh, is your wife here, Rudy?" laughed Harry.

" . . . What?" asked Rudy.

"Is your wife here, Rudy?"

" . . . What?"

"Heh, heh, heh," chuckled Harry, "Uh . . . oh, by the way . . . is your wife here, Rudy? We'd love to meet her."

"She's in the bathroom," replied Rudy. He walked over to the bathroom door and opened it just enough to stick his head inside.

"Aunt Tillie and Uncle Harry are here, darling."

Rudy made a high, sing-song squeal, as if it was Annie's voice answering him. Then he turned back to the family.

"She says to say hello."

Harry wasn't sure what he'd heard. The rest of the family reacted as if they were allowed to visit an insane asylum if they remained quiet.

"She went into the bathtub," said Rudy. "She wants to freshen up a little bit and then meet us later. Is that all right?"

"Certainly, certainly," said Harry. "She sounds like a charming girl."

"Oh! . . . Here are your things, darling." Rudy picked up Annie's robe from the floor and stuck his head and hands inside the bathroom again.

"I love you, too!" shouted Rudy from inside the bathroom, "Oh, yes! Just as much as you do. Oh, yes, I do!"

Rudy backed out of the bathroom, smiling broadly and wiping "lipstick" off of his mouth.

Uncle Harry looked at Tillie in disbelief. "Well . . . how are you, Rudy?"

"Wonderful. Wonderful," said Rudy, almost crying. "Oh, God, I'm so happy. Look! How do you like my swimming pool?" Rudy dove full-length into the water and started to dog-paddle. The family just stood there, their mouths gaping.

"Oh boy! Isn't this something? Would you like to take a little dip?" Rudy asked.

"Heh, heh, heh, heh," laughed Harry, looking at the water. "He's on the borderline," Harry whispered to his wife. Then he rolled up his trouser legs and jumped full-length into the water. "Oh, this is delightful," he said.

"There are only four rooms like this in the whole hotel," said Rudy, as he started to do laps.

"No kidding," said Harry. "Get in the water, Tillie."

"*What?*" asked Tillie's frightened eyes.

Uncle Harry pointed to his head and then muttered, "He's south of the border. I don't want to embarrass him, you get my meaning? Now get in the water . . . all of you."

The whole family, fully clothed, waded into the water.

"All right now, kids," said Harry. "Stay away from the deep end unless you're with a grownup." He started to breaststroke alongside Rudy. "Oh boy! This is the life. You having fun, Rudy?"

"Wonderful!" said Rudy.

"Good. Oh, by the way . . . how are you feeling about your screen test? Not too nervous, are you?"

"No . . . no. I'm fine," Rudy had forgotten all about it.

"That's a boy. Well, we can't stay that long, Rudy. I just wanted to meet Annie and bring you the record from Rainbow Studios."

"A record?" asked Rudy.

"Yes. In that cardboard box on the table. They said it was for you to practice your acting. Okay, kids . . . Let's get ready to go."

The kids were really having fun. Aunt Tillie just waded, gently, trying to keep her hem from getting wet.

"Aw," chanted the kids.

"Come on! Your fingers look like prunes. Three more dives and that's it. The screen test is at one o'clock sharp, Rudy."

"One o'clock today?" asked Rudy, astonished.

"That was it. They said take it or leave it. All right . . . everybody out now!"

"Aw, Dad," the kids chanted.

"I said out! Your lips are turning blue! If the hotel doesn't have a phonograph," he said to Rudy, "there's a Liberty Music Shop just around the corner." Uncle Harry and the family climbed out of the water, their clothes completely soaked. "Oh, that was refreshing. That really hit the spot. Well, I'll be back for you at twelve thirty, all right, Rudy?"

"Yes," said Rudy. He had stopped swimming.

"Okay! Keep up the good work. Just relax. You gotta relax! Oh . . . *Goodbye, Annie!*"

Rudy quickly turned his back and made another high, squealing sound, as if Annie were answering.

"Heh, heh, heh, heh, heh. You've got a lovely girl there, Rudy. You're a lucky fellow. See you at twelve thirty."

After the family left, Rudy sat down in the water, a glassy stare in his eyes.

Downstairs, the hotel manager was registering a very wealthy elderly couple into the hotel.

"Oh, you won't have to worry about that, madam. We have only the finest clientele. Kings, queens . . . the crème de la crème."

Just then, Uncle Harry and his dripping wet family walked past, leaving a soggy trail behind them.

"What the hell kind of hotel do you run here? It's too hot, you hear me? Too goddamn hot!" he shouted.

The hotel manager could hardly speak. "I'll have your bags sent up to your room."

People in the lobby stared at the family as they walked out of the hotel with great dignity. The manager banged his head on the small bell in front of him to ring for a porter.

CHAPTER 10

ANNIE STOOD WITH HER small suitcase and her coat over her arm, gazing at the Paramount Pictures gate. The taxi made a U-turn and disappeared. "The home of Rudolph Valentino," she thought as she stared at the magnificent white arch that separated Paramount from the rest of the world. Annie thought of her home in Milwaukee and of Rudy. Then she took a deep breath and started to walk through the gate.

"Hey! *Hey!* Where ya goin', honey?"

Annie looked at the guard who suddenly stood in front of her. "I have an appointment to see Mr. Valentino," she said.

The guard checked his board. "What's your name?" he asked.

Annie just stood there, gazing way off into the distance.

"Excuse me, dear . . . what's your name? I have to check it on this list," he said very patiently.

"I don't think it's there," replied Annie.

The guard smiled. This was just another girl trying to get in to see the great star.

"I can't let you in unless it is, Ma'am," he said sympathetically.

"Oh," Annie said. Her face dropped. The kindly guard noticed and tried to comfort her. She looked so forlorn.

"Why don't you tell me your name?" he asked, "Maybe it is here."

"Mrs. Valen . . ." but she suddenly stopped. From out of nowhere, a huge studio van screeched up and stopped. On the side of the van was a giant photograph of Rudolph Valentino.

". . . tine," Annie continued, half consciously.

"Tine? Wait a minute. What did you say your name was? Mrs. what?"

Annie looked up at the poster of Valentino. He seemed to be smiling at her.

"Mrs. Valentino," she said.

"Oh," gasped the guard. "Well . . . Jesus . . . I'm sorry, Ma'am. Do you mind if I just call, uh…" The guard looked up at the face of Valentino, who gave him a chilling stare. "Oh, to hell with it. Go ahead, dear. He's usually on Stage Six."

The van started forward. "Thank you," Annie

said as she followed Valentino through the awe-some gates of Paramount.

Rudy waded through the still-flooded sunken living room. He was naked from his undershorts down, but he had on his best suit, shirt, tie and hat. He carried his pants, shoes and socks above his head.

Just as he was in the middle of the room, a large maid with a bucket and mop knocked on the door and walked in. She stared at Rudy, waist-high in the water.

"Oh, good," said Rudy, ad-libbing rapidly. "You're just in time. There seems to be a small leak in the bathroom. Would you be kind enough to tell the manager for me, please? I'd like to have it repaired by the time I get back." He climbed out of the water and dripped his way to the door, picking up the audition record on his way out.

"Thank you very much," he said as he exited.

The maid just stared. She looked at the gallons of water and then at her humble bucket and mop.

Downstairs, directly below the bedroom, a headwaiter walked past a man and a woman seated at a table eating breakfast.

"Oh, waiter," the man said, "may we have some water, please?"

"Certainly, sir," the waiter said, snapping his fingers. At that moment, a piece of the ceiling caved in, flooding the dumbfounded couple with water.

A captain rushed up, furious with the head-waiter.

"Clean up this mess," he screamed.

The dazed headwaiter snapped his fingers again and the large maid, still with her bucket and mop, crashed onto the center of the table from above. The captain and the drenched couple looked at the headwaiter. The astonished waiter looked at his fingers.

Annie walked through the streets of Paramount, overwhelmed by the lavish street sets and the crowds of extras dressed in exotic clothes. It was a warm, sunny California day and all the stage doors were open. Suddenly she heard a woman let out a piercing scream. Annie timidly peeked into the stage where the sound had come from. Inside was a lavish French revolution set and Marie Antoinette was kneeling in front of a guillotine. She screamed again as the blade fell, her dismembered head falling into a basket.

"*Cut*," the director yelled casually, and the mob of extras immediately began to disperse. The headless Marie Antoinette got up from the guil-lotine and lifted a flap in her costume just below her neck. The face of a small man poked through and lit a cigarette as two prop men started to reat-tach the fake head onto his shoulders.

Annie backed quietly out of the stage. As she turned her head, she saw two enormous camels coming straight towards her. She tried to jump

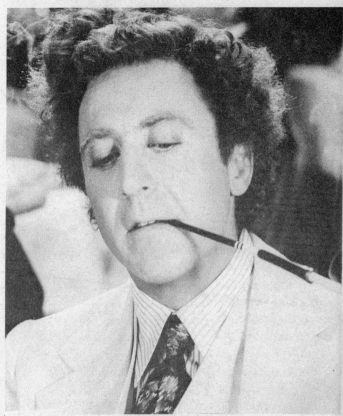
Gene Wilder, writer, director and star of
The World's Greatest Lover.

Gene Wilder and co-star Carol Kane.

Dom De Luise as movie mogul Adolph Zitz.

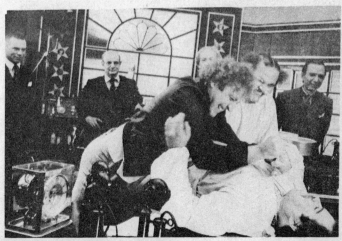

Gene Wilder directs Dom De Luise in
the gentle art of training a barber.

Legionnaires guarding the most precious
sight in a desert—an oasis.

Gene Wilder demonstrates the proper way
to seduce your wife.

Richard Dimitri, as Tony Lassiter, looks on as
Gene Wilder sets up the scene.

Gene Wilder, Carol Kane, and friends.

Gene Wilder plays Rudy Hickman, a perpetual
daydreamer who fancies himself the next Valentino.

Rudy has trouble keeping up with
his work in the pastry shop.

Rudy realizes that baking cakes is
not his true vocation . . .

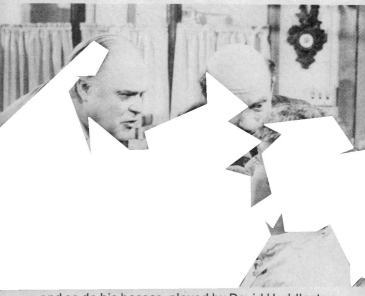

. . . and so do his bosses, played by David Huddleston (left), and Charles Knapp.

Rudy has a strange nervous habit!

Rudy changes his last name to Valentine and
boards a train to California.

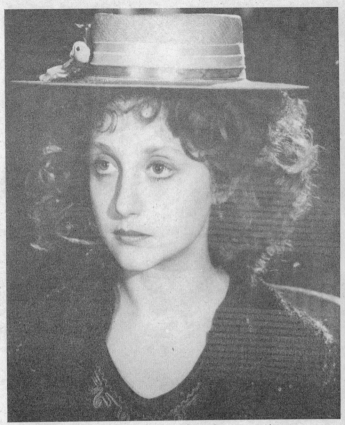

Carol Kane as Rudy's wife Annie, who secretly
worships the great Rudolph Valentino.

Rudy and Annie arrive in Hollywood.

Rudy finds a shortcut from his hotel room
to the dance floor below.

Rudy and Annie face marital difficulties.

Rudy enjoys an after-dinner swim in
his sunken living room.

Matt Collins as Rudy's idol, the legendary
Rudolph Valentino.

Rudy and Valentino in an impromptu tango.

A simple tablecloth transforms Rudy Valentine into Rudolph Valentino—or does it?

y and Valentino stumble onto a
xican street festival.

Annie, dressed in a slave girl's costume, enters Valentino's bedchamber.

Rudy, masquerading as Valentino, has an affair with his own wife.

Thinking she has been unfaithful to her husband,
a despondent Annie walks along the beach.

Rudy finds that he can pass for the great Valentino in every way...

. . . but one.

Dancing slave girls bring a touch of
Busby Berkeley to the desert.

At first the reaction to Rudy's audition
is hardly favorable.

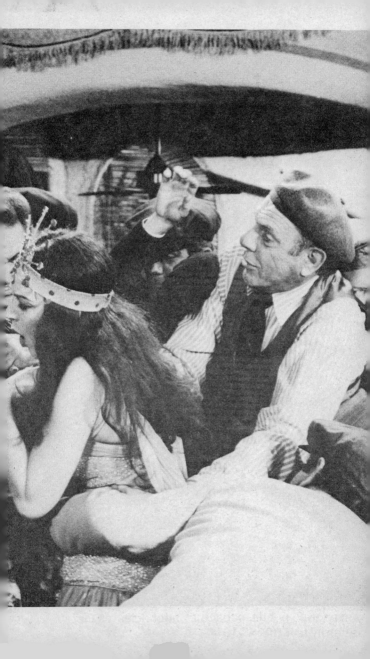

An adoring public mobs Rudy after he earns the title of ''The World's Greatest Lover.''

Reunited at last, Rudy and Annie ride off into the sunset.

back, but the animals walked casually to each side of her, revealing a crowd of actors, all dressed in Arabian costumes, relaxing in the sun. Animals, costumes and props were being loaded onto trucks as an assistant director yelled out orders to the crew.

"I don't want a mess," he shouted. "I do not want a mess here. Careful . . . Slow and easy. Let's not have any mess."

"Excuse me," Annie said to this man who seemed to be in charge. "Could you please tell me where I can find Rudolph Valentino?"

"He could be anywhere around here, lady," said the assistant. "He's probably getting ready to go. You've got a big ass, Chico, and two more horses. So leave some room."

"Go where?" Annie asked, a little shocked.

"What?" said the proccupied assistant.

"Getting ready to go where?" said Annie.

"Location . . . *Aw, Jesus!*"

"Where is that?" Annie persisted.

"They're shitting on the turbans . . . What's the matter with you?" yelled the assistant to a wrangler, who was pulling at a large spotted horse.

"Whaddya want me to do?" asked the wrangler.

"Well, don't let them do it on the turbans. Get 'em outta here."

"Hold your horses," shouted the wrangler.

"You hold *your* horses," the assistant yelled back.

"Where is that?" Annie asked again.

"Where is what?" said the assistant impatiently.

"Location?" said Annie.

"Honey . . . are you packed and ready to go?" asked the assistant.

"Yes," Annie said, clutching her small suitcase.

"Then get on the bus. Just take your bag and get on the blue bus. They'll take you there. Watch your ass, Harry, I'm not kidding."

"Thank you," Annie said. As she started to walk off, she heard the sound of horse's hooves coming towards her. She turned and a man in a sheik's costume reined up sharply. A white sheik's scarf covered his nose and mouth. His eyes fixed on her. Annie stared at the mysterious man. Her heart began to pound. Her throat dried. And then he was gone, galloping off into the distance past the blue bus as people were getting ready to go. Annie stood and watched him disappear around a corner. Then she slowly walked toward the blue bus.

"No, sir. There's nothing here from your wife. No messages at all," the hotel clerk said to Rudy, who was now fully dressed and on his way to try out the audition record.

"Thank you. Uh . . . "

"Yes, sir?" the clerk asked.

"I imagine it's very difficult to meet any of the big movie stars," Rudy said.

"Oh, yes, sir."

"I mean, for instance . . . someone like Rudolph Valentino," Rudy said.

"Oh . . . He'd be surrounded by guards night and day," the clerk replied. "But, of course, you're very famous, Mr. Valentine. You wouldn't have any trouble meeting anyone you wished."

"Yes. Yes, of course. Well . . . thank you." Rudy left for the Liberty Music Shop to play his audition record.

CHAPTER 11

WHEN HE GOT TO THE shop, Rudy waited his turn and then was ushered into a small glass booth, with people on either side of him. He placed his hat on top of a large Victrola horn and his jacket around the back of it. He wanted it to look as human as possible so that he had something to act to. He placed the record on the turntable and a majestic voice came forth.

"Gentlemen! What you are about to hear may be the most important words ever spoken to you in your lifetime. Pretend that you are in makeup and costume. Opposite you is a beautiful woman. Your first direction: look at her with love in your eyes."

Rudy stared at the Victrola horn. He lowered his eyes slightly and gave a teasing little smile.

"Now . . . look at her with love just in your *left* eye," said the record.

Rudy's left eye opened even wider.

"Now switch the love from your left eye to your right eye!"

This was difficult but, after a moment, he mastered the change without losing the feeling.

"All right . . . now let sex ooze from your shoulders."

Rudy was perlexed, but he tried his best.

"Keep letting it ooze, keep letting it ooze . . . now let it ooze right down your chest."

Rudy watched the sex as it oozed down.

"Now say . . . 'Hi! Feel like a dance?'"

Rudy took a deep breath and boldly said the words to the Victrola horn. A woman in the next booth turned around sharply. She thought that Rudy was talking to her.

"The girl stands up. Her lips are two inches from yours."

Rudy was almost cross-eyed. He reacted to everything the imaginary girl in the record was doing, just as if it were being done to him.

"She plays with your right ear. She opens her mouth teasingly. And then she . . . slaps you in the face!"

The woman from the next booth watched Rudy through the glass, but she could not hear the record. All she could do was see Rudy reacting as if someone had spit on his feet, ripped his shirt and socked him in the stomach. She was watching what was obviously a crazy man.

"She throws her drink in your face!" the record went on. "Now, what do you do?"

Rudy drew back, ready to sock the imaginary girl.

"You *laugh!*"

Rudy's fist stopped in midair. He was shocked, but he obeyed.

"Ha!" he said.

"You laugh again," came the direction.

"Ha! Ha!" said Rudy, throwing his head back. Several people turned to look in at Rudy's booth.

"And again!" said the record.

"Ha! Ha! Ha! Ha! Ha!" Rudy laughed.

The whole store full of people had now turned to see what was going on inside Rudy's booth. They started to move in closer to watch a maniac laughing.

"All right . . . the teasing is over . . . . now *show us what a real lover can do!*"

Rudy, hesitantly at first, whipped off his suspenders, dropping his pants around his ankles. He climbed on top of the Victrola horn and began to make love to it. Suddenly he froze. As he turned his head to look out the window, he saw a sea of gasping faces watching with fascination.

Flushed with embarrassment, Rudy quickly pretended that he had a thousand itches on his thighs and knees. He took his hat, put on his jacket and walked out of the back door of the booth, his pants still hanging around his ankles.

As the blue Paramount Pictures bus pulled into the seaside location that afternoon, the cast and crew were in high spirits. They had been singing and eating together on the bus and the whole group had become quite a family.

Annie slipped off the bus and tried to be as inconspicuous as possible. But nobody seemed to notice her anyway. The crew started to erect large tents and unload equipment, and the cast threw off their clothes and ran into the ocean for a quick swim before the sun disappeared.

Annie took off her coat, spread it on the ground, and sat down next to the sea . . . waiting.

CHAPTER 12

THE RAINBOW STUDIOS WAITING room was filled with hundreds of contestants, all dressed in various Arab costumes. Some of them were doing ballet exercises, others practiced their "looks" in front of long mirrors. Some just practiced their laughs which they, too, had been exhorted to learn on their audition records.

Rudy, dressed as a sheik, sat on a bench. Suddenly and uncontrollably, he stuck out his tongue. Another contestant, sitting across from him, thought that Rudy was doing it to him, so he stuck his tongue out at Rudy.

The room suddenly went still as an assistant walked in and checked his board.

"Rudy Valentine!" he shouted.

Rudy snapped out of his trance. He looked towards the voice that had called him.

"You're next, Mr. Valentine."

Rudy got up from the bench. The other sheiks watched him as he slowly made his way towards the door.

The huge stage was dark except for a small concentration of lights way off in the distance. Rudy followed the assistant director towards the lights and, as he got closer, he could see that there was a small set, the semblance of a North African café.

Around the set stood a group of people: cameramen, electricians, script girl, director, producers and others. They all watched Rudy silently as he approached, judging him.

The producer whispered to his secretary and she wrote something in her note pad. The director seemed nervous, fevered. He stared at Rudy intensely. Suddenly, he bolted out of his chair and screamed:

"*Cut!* I mean, uh . . . what am I saying? I'm sorry, I mean . . . hello." The director shook Rudy's hand. "How are you today, Mr. Rudy, uh, Mr. Valentine?"

"Fine," Rudy said.

"Did you get a record to play with—I mean to practice with?" the director asked.

As Rudy nodded "yes", a flash went off. A photographer had taken Rudy's picture. The crew started to get into their positions.

"Good," said the director. He put his arm around Rudy's shoulder. "Mr. Valentine, you understand that this is just the preliminary audition. We're going to pick three men. If you pass today . . . you enter the final audition on Friday. Clear?''

Rudy nodded.

''That a boy. Say hello to Miss Anne Calassandro, who will be your acting partner today.''

A handsome dark-haired woman acknowledged him with a nod.

''Now, Mr. Valentine, if you'll just wait outside that set door there and then when I call the word ''action'' . . . you enter, give the place a quick once-over and walk straight to Miss Calassandro. All right, Rudy? Is that good for you?''

Rudy nodded again.

''Good. This is a hello. No, no, this is a take . . . A take!''

Big lights suddenly flooded the stage. The actress sat down next to a table on the set and held up a fake cocktail. Rudy disappeared outside the door. The clapper boy put a slate in front of the camera lens, as they started to roll. It read:

Director: DORSETT
Test No.: 4,011
Name: Rudy Valentine

''What do you mean, four thousand and eleven?'' asked the director, ''I thought I did four thousand and eighteen screen tests this week.''

''No, sir,'' said his assistant, ''this makes four

thousand and eleven. I promise, I've kept . . . "

"We're falling behind again?" the director interrupted.

"Yes, sir, I'm afraid so, but . . . "

"All right! All right!" interrupted the director. "No big deal. Kiss me."

"I beg your pardon!" said the astonished assistant.

"Kiss me, kiss me."

The assistant gave him a little kiss on the cheek.

"All right!" shouted the director to the crew, "Let's get it over with. If this jerk can act, I'll eat camel shit. Okay, Mr. Valentine . . . this is it. Above all...just have fun and relax. Okay...." The director picked up a bullhorn and held it to his lips.

". . . Action."

Everyone watched the door, but nothing happened.

"I said action, Mr. Valentine."

Rudy burst through the door and stood with his hands on his hips. He circled his head, giving the place a strange kind of once-over, then fixed his eyes on the slave girl. He flared his nostrils and widened his eyes.

The director was not sure exactly what he was looking at, but he carried on.

"Interesting, all right . . . now walk over to the slave girl."

Rudy started to walk.

"Look at her: This is the woman who has just broken your heart. *Annie!*"

When Rudy heard the director call out his wife's name, he froze. Anne Calassandro turned to the director.

"Annie, he's coming nearer . . . this man who saw you only as a little toy without feelings. Rudy . . . here she is . . . that shy, frightened girl whom you took care of like a wounded animal. Now she won't even look at you. Look at her shoulders, Rudy! How many times did you kiss those naked shoulders? Those little ringlets of hair around that angel face? And those breasts, Rudy? For God's sake, don't forget the breasts."

Rudy stared at them.

"Even now—in spite of everything—you long to touch them ever so lightly with your lips. But how many others have played with those same breasts? Squooshed them with their sweaty palms? You were so good to her. And how does she repay you. By running off with another man! Annie . . . look at him. Burn him with your contempt. Rudy . . . don't give her the satisfaction. Don't let her know that your heart is breaking in half. Instead . . . you're cool. Blasé! You say: 'Hi! My name is Felix. Feel like a dance?' Go ahead, Rudy. Just as casual as can be."

"*Whore!*" Rudy yelled and charged towards the surprised actress. Everyone jumped halfway out of their seats as Rudy grabbed her by the throat and started to choke her. Anne stared at him in disbelief.

"Hey! What the fu—" she gasped.

"Telling me Valentino you want Rudolph your touch titties?" Rudy screamed.

Everybody was mesmerized.

"You want to do number eight with Valentino?" Rudy began to drag the choking actress around the room by the throat.

"More seven, more seven, more seven . . . and . . . Now! Good! . . . Yes! I love you, Annie. And eight! Eight! Eight!"

Members of the crew jumped up and tried to pull Rudy off the actress as the director threw his own tantrum.

"I want the name of the person who let this fruitcake onto my set!" he screamed.

"Eight! Eight! Eight! Eight!" Rudy yelled with tears in his eyes. The crowd had now overcome him and was dragging him off.

"Eight! Eight! Eight! Eight!"

The stage door opened and Rudy was thrown out onto the street.

"And don't ever come back, you dumb lunatic!"

CHAPTER 13

TWO SHADOWS STOOD QUIETLY against a wall in a small office off the chapel of St. Anthony's Church. The taller of the two men remained silent as the other, a priest, whispered soothingly to him.

"You such a good boy. If everybody know how much money you give to my little church whenever we in trouble . . . " The silhouette of his hands danced on the wall as he gesticulated with emotion. "But you so modest. No wonder all those girls love you so much."

The other man nodded modestly and prepared to leave. The priest embraced him and thanked him again.

"Grazie tanto. Mille grazies," he said.

"Si, si, si, si," replied the other man. His voice was so quiet he was barely audible. He walked to a coat rack and put on a stylish hat as the priest hurried to a window and peeked out of the blind.

"No!" said the priest. "Too many pretty girls. Somebody must a seen you come in this way. Come on . . . we go out through the chapel."

A few people were praying in the small and beautiful old Mexican chapel. Candles illuminated the backs of their bowed heads as the two men walked slowly up the aisle.

"Not the big door," whispered the priest. "That little door, next to St. Anthony. Nobody gonna be waitin' outside there. Go. Go." The priest squeezed the man's hand and sent him on his way, thanking him again.

"Mille grazies. Mille grazies," he said.

The mysteriously humble man acknowledged the priest with a little backward wave of his hand. He then walked quickly through the small church towards the side door.

"Valentino mumble mumble mumble mumble."

The man stopped. From behind a pillar he thought he heard someone call out his name. He shrugged and continued walking.

"Mumble mumble mumble Rudolph Valentino mumble mumble mumble."

The man stopped again. This time there could be no mistake. He walked towards a side of the chapel where, at a small altar, a man was kneeling in front of the statue of St. Anthony and praying audibly.

"St. Anthony . . . help me. I don't know what to do. I don't want to live anymore. I'm lost. I

think of my little Annie . . . lying down next to
Rudolph Valentino . . . and he's kissing her so
softly . . . the way I never could . . . and I think to
myself: 'Well, if that's what she wants . . . I'll kill
him! I'll kill that son of a bitch.' "

"Oh, God. Forgive me. I just want to die.
Please . . . help me. Show me a sign. One small
signal that you hear me." Rudy buried his head in
his hands, hopelessly deflated.

A finger tapped him on the shoulder. Rudy
turned and looked up at the face of Rudolph Valentino.

Rudy was amazed. He turned his head to the
statue and thanked the saint. Valentino smiled at
him and beckoned him forward with his little finger. Rudy's jaw dropped. He quickly gathered his
things together and followed Valentino out of the
church, whispering a quick "thanks" to the
statue of St. Anthony.

They walked through the back streets of the
quaint Mexican-Italian neighborhood and Rudy
tried calmly to explain his predicament.

Soon Rudy was flailing his arms in the air passionately as he found himself more and more able
to release his emotions. At one point, he almost
choked Valentino as his feelings gushed out. Valentino remained passive as he listened to the
problem, evaluating the dilemma to himself.
Rudy finally broke down. He started to weep on
the great star's shoulder as they walked along the
street.

A small Mexican band played in a restaurant nearby and, as Valentino swung Rudy around to avoid walking into a lamp post, the band struck up the first chord of a dashing tango. As the music played on, Rudy and Valentino unconsciously dipped in time with the music.

As they walked past the restaurant, Valentino pulled at a tablecloth spilling food and dishes on an amazed couple. He quickly made the tablecloth into a scarf around Rudy's nose and mouth. Rudy looked confused. Valentino wrapped the tablecloth around Rudy's head and turned it into an exotic sheik's headgear. He whispered something into Rudy's ear. Rudy shook his head. What Valentino was suggesting was completely out of the question. Valentino started to bounce up and down, as if he were riding a horse. He encouraged Rudy to do the same. Rudy let out a laugh and began to ride his imaginary horse down the street with Valentino. For a brief moment, the great star had given him hope.

The two laughing men rode around a corner and found themselves in a small, local carnival. Music was playing from a bandstand full of brightly dressed Mexican minstrels. Stalls and small shops lined the street and children squashed up close to the toy stalls, hoping that somehow they could have some of the treasures. The street sloped downhill and Rudy and Valentino stopped for a moment to catch their breath. Valentino began to explain another part of his plan to Rudy.

He held an imaginary woman in his arms and threw her down on the ground, then he lay down beside her and whispered in her ear. Rudy again shook his head.

A large old Mexican man emptied a sack of glass marbles onto his stall and the children rushed around at the sight of the new attraction. They became so excited by the brightly colored marbles that they pushed up hard against the stall, knocking it over. The marbles started to roll down the hill towards Rudy and Valentino, who were now walking slowly, very much wrapped up in the plot they were hatching. They didn't notice the marbles coming towards them. The Mexican band quickened its tempo.

Suddenly, the marbles reached the two men's feet and they lurched forward. Strangely, they seemed to slip and slide to the music, as they held each other for support. As they jerked their way down the street in time to the music, astonished onlookers gaped at the amazing couple. Finally, the two men crashed to the ground, laughing and embracing as they rubbed their bruised knees. Rudy had finally accepted the exotic plan of his mortal enemy and loving friend . . . Rudolph Valentino.

CHAPTER 14

"HEY . . . . . IS YOUR NAME Annie Hickman?" a commanding voice came out of the darkness. It was the assistant director who had ushered Annie onto the bus at Paramount. Annie looked up with a jolt. She had been sitting alone in the semidarkness while workers erected tents and set up lights on a long stretch of sand. Annie could hear the sea not more than fifty yards away. A spotlight hit Annie's eyes and blinded her for a moment. She held her hand up to the light and called out to the voice that had called her name.

"Yes."

"Mr. Valentino wants to see you," said the assistant.

"Who?" Annie asked, not believing what she'd heard.

The assistant walked in front of the spotlight, casting a silhouette of himself.

"Rudolph Valentino. He wants to see you in his tent."

"Me?" gasped Annie.

"Yes, you. What are you . . . an extra?" inquired the assistant.

". . . Yes," Annie replied hesitantly.

"It's that great big tent with all the stripes."

The giant structure had taken on a strange, ominous quality in the darkness of the night.

"Thank you," said Annie.

"Why don't you go over to wardrobe and get into a pretty costume," said the assistant. "He might be looking for someone to do a specialty bit."

"Where should I go?" asked Annie.

"That big tent over there on your left."

The spotlight swung along the ground, stopping at a large orange tent.

"Tell them you're supposed to see Mr. Valentino and you want something sexy."

"Thank you," said Annie.

"That's okay. This could be your lucky night. Let's get this show on the road," the assistant yelled out to his crew.

Annie walked to the wardrobe tent and introduced herself to a large Italian lady. The woman gave Annie a scantily made slave dress to try on. It was very revealing. The Italian lady took the front of the dress and gave it a tug, revealing even more bosom. Annie gasped. She started to cover herself in embarrassment. The Italian lady gently pulled away Annie's hands.

"Aw no, honey . . . that's jus' nice. You so pretty, but who knows it if you gonna hide everything," she laughed. Then she gave Annie a big kiss on the cheek and sent her out.

Annie walked towards the large candy-striped tent. She walked past some of the crew, who were moving lights into position for the night shoot. Suddenly, Annie's body was flooded with light as a huge spotlight passed her. Instinctively she covered her chest with her arms. She felt so naked in the slave girl's costume. But the light passed and she was once again in semidarkness. Finally she reached the tent. She held her heart for a moment and then knocked against what seemed to be the door to the tent. Her effort made no sound. She knocked again, harder this time.

"Hi!"

Annie looked up. She had been knocking on the massive chest of Rudolph Valentino's bodyguard.

"Mr. Valentino is expecting you. Come in," the guard said, as he led her into the exotically decorated tent. It was lit by torches, casting lovely shadows, and the floors were covered with lush rugs and huge pillows.

"Make yourself at home," said the bodyguard.

Annie looked around. She decided she would feel more comfortable if she remained standing. The bodyguard walked over to a huge metal gong, picked up a giant mallet, and gonged three times. Annie's eyes widened, not knowing what to expect next. The bodyguard put down the mallet, picked up a violin from a table and disappeared behind a translucent curtain. He was now discreetly separated from the bedchamber and he began to play a hauntingly romantic tune on the violin.

Annie suddenly heard a horse approaching. She turned quickly towards the rear of the tent. Suddenly there appeared a sheik, dressed in black silk, a scarf covering his mouth and nose. He rode through the opening of the tent and reined up sharply. His eyes stared at Annie. She stared back at the person she thought was Rudolph Valentino.

The rider flung his right leg expertly over the saddle and did an extraordinarily cool dismount. But his belt was stuck onto the protruding horn of his Arabian saddle and, as he tried to slide off the magnificent horse, he dangled in midair. The horse turned around and carried Rudy back out of the tent.

Annie was a little confused. The bodyguard stopped playing and stepped out from behind the curtain to see what was going on. Rudy quickly reappeared, on foot, through the back of the tent and the bodyguard stepped back behind his curtain and began to play again. Rudy regained his cool as he approached Annie. He spoke in a high tenor voice, affecting an Italian accent.

"Hullo. I'm Rudolph Valentino. How you been?"

"Fine, thank you," replied Annie.

"Oh, my . . . don't you look nice. Say, did you write me a lot of letters?" asked Rudy.

"Yes, I did."

"Oh yeah, I remember. Say! What you like about me so much, huh? I mean I jus' wanna know."

"Well . . . " said Annie, a little embarrassed, "You're so . . . sympathetic."

"Oh, yeah. Yeah," agreed Rudy.

"And . . . " Annie continued, "you seem to be very understanding. I think you know what goes on in a woman's heart."

" . . . Yeah, I got that. That's right. But you forgettin' one very big thing," said Rudy.

"What?" asked Annie, innocently.

"I'm a sissy boy."

The music stopped playing. From behind the curtain, the bodyguard gaped with confusion. Annie's eyes widened with disbelief.

"What . . . what are you saying?"

"Oh, yeah," said Rudy in his high-pitched voice. "I like a nice guy sometimes. It's a lotta fun."

"You?" asked an amazed Annie. "That can't be true. I don't believe it."

"You don't believe me! Okay," said Rudy. He called out to the bodyguard. "Oh, say there, handsome . . . come on out here a minute."

The bodyguard stepped out from behind the curtain.

"Let's see one of your legs," said Rudy.

The bodyguard looked at Rudy strangely.

"Come on," said Rudy. "Let's have a little peek."

The bodyguard hesitantly pulled up the loose bloomer pants around one of his long hairy legs. Rudy let out a sharp whistle and a couple of woofs.

"Look at those gams. Now that's what I call good-looking," he said.

"It can't be true. Please. Tell me you're only teasing me," Annie said.

Rudy continued to devote his affections to the bodyguard. "What you doin' tonight, honey? Maybe we could meet later for a little snack." He let out another whistle.

Having heard his usual whistle, Valentino's horse charged into the tent, right in between Rudy and Annie.

"Get outta here!" Rudy yelled to the horse.

"Oh, no," gasped Annie. The whole dilemma overtook her and she fainted. The confused horse charged back out of the tent. Rudy rushed over to her, propping her head up onto a pillow. He thought she'd been knocked over by the horse.

"Annie! What happened? Oh, my God," Rudy yelled in his own voice. He was so overcome by all the turmoil that he had completely forgotten his role.

"What did you say?" Annie asked, waking suddenly.

"I say," Rudy said in his high tenor voice again, "Annie! What happened? Oh, my God!"

Annie looked at him with love in her eyes.

"Take me!" she said.

Rudy froze. He'd never heard those words from her before. It had always been he who had had to initiate their lovemaking. His lifelong nervous habit took control of him and his tongue stuck out. All Annie could see, though, was the black scarf across Rudy's mouth jut out for a moment. She sat up. From all the jostling, her shoulders had become even more exposed.

"Take me! Please . . . take me," she begged.

"Where?" asked Rudy.

"Oh, you! You're only fooling again. You didn't mean that about liking boys . . . did you?" she asked coyly.

"Well . . . " Rudy croaked. Now his laryngitis had returned and he quickly tried to recover.

"I mean: 'Well' . . . " but he'd said that in his own voice, not the high-pitched squeak that he'd been pretending.

"I mean: 'Well' . . . "

"Oh, stop!" Annie said. Rudy thought he'd given the game away. "You're just trying to tease me again. I know that you like girls. You love them . . . don't you?" Annie asked sensuously.

"Well, maybe once a month," Rudy replied.

"Oh, no . . . you can't fool me anymore. Would you like me to tell you who you really are?"

That was it. Rudy's tongue jutted out through his scarf and he began to talk with his stifled laryngitis again.

"Who?" he croaked.

"I mean: 'Who?' " he said in his high tenor voice.

"I mean: 'Who?' " he said in a normal voice.

"I mean: 'Who?' " he said in a high tenor voice again. He was totally lost.

"You're the world's greatest lover . . . aren't you?" Annie asked. She touched her husband's eyebrows affectionately. "Aren't you?" she asked again teasingly.

Rudy looked at Annie's bare shoulders. His jealousy of Valentino was mixed with the strangest feeling of passion he had ever known.

"You must have had other men who gave you happiness?" he asked.

"No," said Annie.

"Well . . . just one man who made you happy . . . once in a while?"

"No," said Annie.

"You mean . . . there wasn't one time, in your whole life, when someone made you happy . . . in *that* way?"

"Never!" replied Annie.

Rudy was crushed. His eyes began to cloud over and his guilt and sorrow drained everything from him.

"My dearest," said Annie, touching his face lightly, "My sweetheart . . . my perfect love . . ."

She closed her eyes and offered her lips to be kissed. "You're the only man I want."

Rudy slapped her across the face and sent her sprawling. He rose like a seething volcano.

"What . . . what happened? What did I do?" she was petrified. Rudy just stared at her, his eyes filled with tears and anger. Annie grabbed a pillow and tried to cover herself. She backed away from Rudy. "What do you want?" she asked.

Rudy put his hands on his hips and grinned behind his mask.

"Oh, no! Wait! I . . . oh, I forgot . . . I have an appointment," she stammered. Rudy advanced toward her. He took off his cape and flung it away.

"Oh, my God! Stop! Please! I've changed my mind," Annie yelled. She had backed herself into a corner. Rudy kept coming towards her.

"You don't understand . . . this isn't what I expected."

Rudy grabbed the pillow that Annie was covering her bosom with and threw it away. Annie screamed. She stood as if she was naked, trying to cover herself with her hands.

Rudy picked her up into his arms.

"Oh, dear God in heaven, have mercy on me," Annie gasped. Rudy smiled lasciviously and, although Annie couldn't see his mouth, she saw the beacons of lust shining through his eyes. The violin began to play wildly. Rudy carried his wife towards a bed of cushions.

CHAPTER 15

THE BLACK AND WHITE image of Rudy danced on the faces of Adolph Zitz and his yes-men. It was the early part of his ill-fated screen test and they all watched with subdued boredom.

"This guy looks like a creep. All right . . . " said Zitz, the barber sitting quietly next to him, manicuring the mogul's nails, "now listen to me. We've got two beauties so far. If we find one more guy in the rest of today's junk that we all agree I really love . . . okay! If not . . . we'll go into the finals with just the two actors we've got. I wouldn't be un—" Suddenly Zitz noticed Rudy go crazy on the screen. "What the hell's going on?"

Rudy was choking Anne Calassandro on the screen, his eyes flaring and popping wildly. The small group watched the screen, amazed at the sight of Rudy being dragged off by the entire crew. A solemn hush filled the air as the screen test ended and the house lights came up.

Zitz sat, stunned, as the barber continued to manicure the mogul's nails. Zitz looked at the director, who sat near him.

"Sorry, Mr. Zitz. This got in by mistake. As I understand it, the man had just last week been released from an insane asylum . . . poor devil. But anyway, that's not your . . . " The director was interrupted by Zitz.

"Whaddya think?" he asked the first yes-man.

"Embarrassing! What can I say?"

"Whaddya think?" Zitz asked another yes-man.

"It was terrible, Mr. Zitz," he replied.

"Whaddya think?" asked Zitz, to the third yes-man.

"Terrible! Terrible! It was just . . . terrible."

"Whaddya think?" asked Zitz, pointing to the barber.

The barber tried to pass his turn on to the fourth yes-man, but Zitz would have none of it.

"No, *you!* What did *you* think?"

"Well, uh . . . terrible," the barber answered cautiously.

"Were you going to say something?" asked Zitz.

"No! I, uh . . . No, no . . . I was just . . . I thought it was terrible."

"Please! You started to say something," Zitz persisted. "I would like very much to hear it."

All the other men in the room lowered their heads. The barber carefully put away all his sharp manicuring instruments. He quickly drank the soapy manicure water and put the finger bowl into his case. He began to twitch as he spoke.

"Oh, I just . . . I . . . but what do I know about these things? These men . . . " he said, pointing to the yes-men. "Anyway, it's just . . . what can I say?" Finally, after he'd put away all sharp or heavy objects that could possibly hurt him, the barber said, "Anyway, I liked him."

Suddenly, Zitz grabbed the barber, who had tried to cover his head.

"*I love this man!*" shouted Zitz. "I want this man by my side sixteen hours a day, every single day of the week . . . is that understood?"

The barber fainted. Zitz went on talking as he carried the barber around the room. He whispered to one of the yes-men, "Make arrangements with his family."

"Gentlemen . . . one of the three actors we saw this week is going to be The World's Greatest Lover. Now—let's get ready for the finals." Zitz kissed the sleeping barber as the yes-men got busy.

CHAPTER 16

SUNSHINE FLOODED THE tent the next morning as Annie dressed behind the translucent curtain. Rudy watched Annie's silhouette as she wiggled a piece of clothing over her head. She hummed softly.

"I want you to know that that was the most wonderful experience I ever had in my life."

Rudy sat, stunned, as he watched the beautiful form of her little body through the screen. Sunlight peeked through the seams in the tent.

"I never knew what lovemaking meant before. Is it like that for you all the time?" Annie asked.

Rudy let out a noncommittal "mmm" through the moist scarf that still covered his face.

"How could you know so much about women?"

Rudy shrugged, not even trying to answer.

"I love you, Rudy."

Rudy looked up. Did she mean Valentino or him? Annie's silhouette turned and faced Rudy.

"Did you hear what I said? I said I love you, Mr. Valentino."

Rudy raised his arms to God. Annie stepped out from behind the curtain.

"Hello," she said.

Rudy tried to make sense of his upraised arms by leaning against a tent pole, which then crashed into the giant gong as a section of the tent collapsed above him.

Suddenly the bodyguard, a makeup man and two dressers rushed in. They all seemed very busy. The makeup man had his case and collapsible chair and the dressers carried in new costumes. They all dropped their things and untangled Rudy from the tent.

"Yes, sir, we was waiting for your signal," the makeup man said. He turned to the bodyguard. "Giovanni, fix the tent up again for Mr. Valentino."

The bodyguard started to fix the tent pole as Annie watched the two dressers lead Rudy to the makeup chair.

"Bring him right over here, boys," said the makeup man. "That's right. You just sit down here, Mr. Valentino, and make yourself comfortable, we gonna fix you up."

Rudy sat in the makeup chair. Half his head was covered by his sheik's headgear. The makeup man pulled a rope which opened a sun flap, illuminating

Rudy's face, just as if makeup lights had been turned on.

"Okay, young lady," said the makeup man. "Time to go home now. Mr. Valentino's gotta get ready to act in the moving pictures." The makeup man hummed lightly under his breath as he pulled off Rudy's headgear, revealing that Rudy was wearing a black Valentino hairpiece.

Annie was stunned by everything that was happening. The makeup man patted a whitish powder over Rudy's entire face.

"We just powder you down a little bit and fix the eyebrows, okay, Mr. Valentino?" the makeup man said. He gave Rudy a secret wink as one of the dressers pulled off Rudy's boots and black tights.

"Oh, Miss! Young lady girl!" said the makeup man. "Mr. Valentino can't play with you no more. You gotta go home now."

Annie just stood there.

"Oh, say," said the makeup man to Rudy, "Today is your big scene where you kill all the bad guys, ain't it, Mr. Valentino?" He gave Rudy another wink as Annie walked over to Rudy.

"Mr. Valentino . . . I don't understand. We just . . . a few minutes ago, we just . . . ." She stood there, aghast. As one of the dressers passed her on his way out, he gave her a little pat on her behind.

"Go on, honey," he said to her, "They've got some nice hot coffee outside."

". . . You said . . . " gasped Annie, her eyes flooding with tears.

One of the dressers called out to Rudy and gave him a sly wink. "Oh, Mr. Valentino . . . that pretty girl you wanted to see about a specialty bit will be in your tent as soon as we break for lunch."

"You said . . . you felt the same way as I did," said Annie.

The makeup man penciled Rudy's already exaggerated eyebrows. "Oh, boy, Mr. Valentino . . . you better get a lotta rest before you audition any more girls." He started to laugh and all the other men joined in. Rudy sat motionless, staring at himself in the mirror. Annie stared at him hoping to see some answer in his powdered eyes. Then she turned and fled from the tent. Rudy's heart sank. Perhaps that was the last time he would ever see her.

Once Annie was gone, the makeup man and one of the dressers scooted Rudy out of the chair and handed him his street clothes.

"Okay, come on, come on, Mr. Hickman," said the makeup man. "Hurry up now. Mr. Valentino's been waiting to come in here all morning. Not nice to take advantage of him. Tony, get Mr. Hickman's shoes and tell Mr. Valentino whenever he's done shooting he can come back to his tent now. I'll get some water for his bath. Hurry, Mr. Hickman. Hurry!" The makeup man left the first dresser to help Rudy back into his own clothes. Rudy stood there with his white face and penciled eyebrows, half naked and half sheik.

CHAPTER 17

ANNIE WANDERED AIMLESSLY along the beach. The hem of her slave girl costume and her sandals got soaked each time the surf came in, but she didn't seem to notice. Neither did she care about the people who were working around her, who had stopped for a moment and watched her disappear over a sand dune.

Annie found herself walking along the coast high road as a distant truck approached. The truck driver was astonished at the sight of Annie, dressed as a slave girl, thumbing a lift. Filled with surprise and the expectation of an adventure, he pulled up and opened the passenger door of his cab.

"I'm goin' downtown L.A., is that all right?" he asked. Annie nodded.

"Hop in, toots. You sure are a cute hitchhiker."

Later on, as they approached downtown, the atmosphere in the cab was very strained. The truck driver had made advances towards Annie, thinking she was "easy" because of the way she was dressed. Annie asked to be let out. The driver pulled over.

"Watch yourself, honey. This is a bad neighborhood."

The truck pulled away, leaving Annie desperate and alone. She began to wander again, with no particular idea where she was going.

She found herself in a particularly sleazy part of Los Angeles, filled with winos and tarts. She became tired and walked up to a pole and rested against it.

"Does the bus stop here?" she asked a passerby.

"Yeah, it'll come," the man replied. He walked on, but looked back with interest at the pretty girl with the strange costume. Annie just stared off into space, leaning against the pole.

"Get in line!" came a voice. Annie heard the remark, but decided it wasn't meant for her.

"Hey!" the voice shouted again. Annie looked around at four whores who were leaning against a building.

"Get in line. We were here first," one of them shouted. Annie looked up at the top of the pole and saw the words "Bus Stop" printed clearly on the sign. Assuming all the girls were waiting for the bus, she walked over and became number five in line.

From around the corner came a tall Mexican gangster, wearing what he considered to be a good suit and hat. Behind him was his short, greasy sidekick, who was trying, with every step, to emulate his boss. They walked up to the first whore and the big man motioned with his head for her to speak.

"Six dollars," the big woman replied.

"Don't waste my time," the gangster retorted. They moved on to the next one in line.

"How much?" he asked.

"Five dollars," she replied.

"Five dollars?" he said. "You ought to buy yourself a mirror," said the gangster. As they moved toward the next girl, the little sidekick noticed Annie at the end of the line. She was just his size.

"How much?" the gangster asked the third whore.

"Three-fifty."

"Bargain day. You givin' away free dishes, too?" They moved on, the sidekick still watching Annie closely. His mouth began to water.

"How much?" asked the gangster, this time to a huge, very fancily dressed whore.

"Eight dollars," she replied. "Eight dollars! Eight dollars? Jesus Christ. Nobody is worth eight dollars. I wouldn't give eight dollars for the Queen of Sheba!" The gangster muttered something under his breath in Spanish and moved on to Annie. By now the sidekick was doing eye rolls for her benefit and it was only then that she realized what was happening.

"How much?" the gangster asked.

"Two thousand dollars!" Annie replied.

The gangster smiled.

"What can you do for two thousand dollars?" he asked.

Annie's mind raced.

"I can do number eight," she said.

The gangster looked at his sidekick and they started to chuckle.

"Can you give me a little sample of number eight?" he laughed.

Annie was lost. She thought of Rudy, of Valentino using her and then throwing her out of the tent. Instead of screaming or swearing, she hit the man as hard as she could in the stomach.

The blow didn't faze the big man at all.

"That's pretty good," he said, grinning insanely. "But I don't think it's worth two thousand dollars. Ain't you got something else for me?"

Annie suddenly drew back and slugged him, but this time a little lower. His expression immediately changed to one of horror and his eyes closed with pain. As he fell to one side, the sidekick stepped in quickly to grab Annie. Once again she drew back and with surprising strength socked the little man full on the chin, almost knocking him off his feet.

Suddenly a policeman's whistle blew and all the whores scattered as five policemen rushed in. But Annie continued to pulverize the sidekick, her eyes wild, as she finally released her emotions.

CHAPTER 18

THE SOUND OF THE HEAVY cell door clanging shut echoed along the cold prison corridors.

The girls in the cells started to shout and whistle as they heard footsteps coming towards them. The jailer's keys rattled rhythmically.

Rudy, unshaven and glassy-eyed, stared at the row of whores hanging on their cell bars, reaching out to touch him. Their makeup seemed even more exaggerated by the harsh overhead lights.

Rudy and the jailer walked past the line of cells, stopping at the last one. Annie sat on a cot. She'd been given an old gray "lost and found" overcoat to keep her warm and it hung loosely around her shoulders.

"Is that her?" the jailer asked.

Rudy nodded.

"We found your husband for you, lady," the jailer said as he opened Annie's cell door. "Okay, mister, she's all yours." He swung the door open and then, sensing the tension, he tactfully made himself scarce.

Rudy walked into the cell, carrying a package wrapped in brown paper and tied with string.

"I brought you some fresh clothes," he said. Annie didn't look at him. She just stared at the floor. Rudy looked at Annie and the cell. Then he, too, stared at the floor.

"I ran off with Rudolph Valentino," Annie said, suddenly breaking the silence. "I made love with him in his tent, and then he threw me out. They were right to send me here. I'll leave you alone, Rudy . . . I promise. You were the only decent thing that ever happened to me." Tears started to well up in her eyes. "If you could just give me enough money to get back to Milwaukee, I'll . . . "

"Forgive me!" Rudy yelled as he dropped to his knees. "Please! Annie! Forgive me!" his voice echoed through the corridors as he buried his face in her lap. Annie instinctively held his head, but she was completely baffled.

Suddenly, the voice of the Poinsettia Hotel manager came booming along the corridor.

"Mr. Valentine! Mr. Valentine!" he shouted as he reached Annie's cell. He was puffing terribly. An ornate black coat with fur lapels was buttoned the wrong way over his silk pajamas. "I just spoke with Mr. Adolph Zitz. You are in the final audition for *The World's Greatest Lover*."

Rudy and Annie looked up at the crazy Hungarian, his eyes popping with excitement. "Rainbow Studios has been trying to reach you all night. Oh . . . hello, madam."

Annie's tearful face broke into a broad smile. "Hello," she said.

"Pardon me," the manager said. "Are you in the middle of . . . rehearsing a little scene?"

"Yes," Annie said.

"Charming. Mr. Zitz called me himself this morning . . . "

"Wait a minute, wait a minute," the jailer shouted, as he ran up to the manager. "Say! Who are you?"

"Who are you?" replied the manager obediently, then continued talking to Rudy. "Mr. Valentine, it's just you and two other gentlemen . . . "

"I said, who *are* you, sir?" the jailer interrupted again.

"You did not!" said the manager. "You said '*Say* who are you?' "

"Well, what *did* you say?" asked the jailer.

"I said, 'who are you?' " replied the manager.

"Say," said the confused jailer, "who the hell *are* you?"

"All right . . . 'who the hell are you?' "

"I said who the hell are you, mister?" The jailer was fast losing his patience.

"You did not! You said '*Say*, who the hell are you?' "

"And what did you say?" the jailer asked.

"I said 'Who the hell are you?' "

That was it. The baffled jailer finally exploded into an enormous rage.

"Say! You'd better tell me your name, mister . . ."

"All right! But this is the last time! 'You'd better tell me your name, mister.' What the hell kind of crazy people they got around here?"

Rudy and Annie sat quietly, looking at each other. Rudy's mind was racing back and forth between the tears in Annie's eyes and the images conjured up by the hotel manager's news.

CHAPTER 19

PREPARATIONS FOR THE final auditions were well under way as Adolph Zitz and his trusty yes-men inspected the finishing touches. The shell-shocked barber had somehow adopted the appearance of his mogul boss, his hair having fallen out in almost an identical pattern. The same peculiar growth, which Zitz called his mustache, also adorned the barber's upper lip. He occasionally sucked his thumb because he found it soothing.

Twenty dancing slave girls lay on their backs in two rows of ten, doing scissor kicks, as a film crew watched from a platform over the girls' heads, setting up one of the shots for the opening sequence of *The World's Greatest Lover*.

Zitz wheeled his barber past them and nodded approvingly. The yes-men followed, also nodding at the scene and catching an interesting eyeful of the lovely girls' legs as they waved them in the air.

At the studio gate, Rudy was getting directions from the guard as Annie sat quietly in the taxi cab. Rudy finished with the guard and ran back over to the cab. Sticking his head through the window, he pleaded:

"Please?"

"No, no, no. I mustn't, Rudy," Annie said. "You have to trust me. I know you'll be so nervous that I'd just make you more nervous."

Rudy looked at her, somehow hoping that she would change her mind, but what she'd said made too much sense.

"You're late, Mr. Valentine," the guard said.

Rudy looked around at him anxiously.

"Please, it's better this way," Annie said.

"All right," Rudy conceded. He leaned forward and they kissed. "You'll be at the hotel?"

"I'll be at the hotel," she said, trying to relax him. "Don't worry about anything."

"They're waiting, Mr. Valentine," said the guard.

Rudy leaned forward and kissed her again. "Bye-bye," he said.

"Bye-bye."

"I'll see you at the hotel?"

"See you at the hotel."

They glanced at each other for a moment, then Rudy turned on his heels and ran through the studio gate.

"Rudy!" shouted Annie.

He stopped in his tracks and turned.

"You can do anything. I promise."

Rudy gave a silly smile and shrugged his shoulders. He turned and sped off towards the audition stage. Annie leaned out of the cab window and watched him disappear around a corner, then she climbed out of the taxi.

"Excuse me," she said to the driver, "I won't be a moment." She walked over to the guard. "Do you have a piece of paper I could write a note on, please?"

"Sure, dear. Just a second."

"Ladies and gentlemen," Zitz shouted. He was surrounded by hundreds of members of the press and radio, photographers, plus twenty Arab soldiers, three slave girls, and the whole production crew. Their talking and laughing suddenly died down as the studio boss' voice thundered across the giant stage.

"In a couple of minutes, you're going to see three auditions. Each man was given the exact same scene this morning to improvise in his own words. Right after the last audition, I'm going to pick the winner, and then . . . just as I promised . . . you're going to watch the winner film his very first scene from Rainbow Studios' new spectacular film, *The World's Greatest Lover!*"

The whole audience broke into excited applause as the tiny tyrant's speech reached its planned crescendo. He waved and smiled while flashbulbs popped, basking in the opportunity to be a star himself.

"All right," he shouted, making the audience die down again. "Take a look at these three faces."

Everybody turned to look at the small café set that was to be used for the auditions, as it was suddenly bathed with light from spotlights high above the stage. There stood the three contestants, dressed as sheiks. They seemed a little startled by the sudden burst of lights.

"Here they are: the three contestants. Examine them closely," said Zitz. The lights directed their beams at the first contestant. A tall, dark, hairy man, with piercing black eyes.

"Form your own opinions. Because in a little while . . ." The lights rotated to the second contestant, a dark, really good-looking man with a moustache.

". . . One of these three men is going to be . . . " The spotlights finally settled on Rudy, staring at the ground and looking very nervous.

". . . The most famous actor in America."

Rudy's tongue came flying out.

CHAPTER 20

AT THE RAINBOW STUDIOS gate, a runner on a bicycle peddled past the guard, on his way to the audition stage. Suddenly, the guard ran out with an envelope.

"Freddie!" he shouted and the runner circled back.

"This is for a guy named Rudy Valentine, on Stage Fourteen."

The runner snatched the envelope and started to peddle off.

"Don't give it to him until after the auditions are over," shouted the guard.

"Gotcha!" said the runner.

The giant stage echoed with applause as the first contestant and his slave-girl partner bowed and smiled after completing their audition. It was always difficult being the first, but he knew he'd given a good performance. One that would be difficult to beat. The director pushed his way through the applauding crowd and congratulated him on his performance.

Adolph Zitz sat in a high chair, a chocolate milk shake and cookies in front of him and his entourage surrounding him. He leaned over to his producer, sitting to his left (in a lower chair, of course), and waited for a response.

"Good, Adolph. Very good," he said encouragingly. The mogul turned to his right, where the barber sat in his wheelchair.

"So? Whaddya think?" he asked, almost a little frightened.

The barber nodded politely. He wasn't that impressed. Zitz muttered something foul under his breath, then motioned to the director to get on with the next audition.

"And now, ladies and gentlemen," called out the director, "our next contestant: Mr. Tony Lassiter."

Flashbulbs began to pop and several people wrote the name down as the second finalist appeared. The director went to greet him, but the actor seemed preoccupied with a warm-up exercise that made him wobble and moan. He was obviously a professional.

In the semidarkness, the runner entered the stage door, with Annie's envelope, and tiptoed over to the back of the audition set.

The second slave girl sat in a chair on the set, as Tony Lassiter walked to his position.

"Ready, Tony?" asked the director.

Tony nodded, still finishing his warm-up.

To the side of the set stood Rudy, watching what was going on with fascination, as the director yelled, "And . . . *action!*"

Tony Lassiter immediately slapped a fake cocktail from the slave girl's hand.

"Look at me when I'm talking to you," he roared. "I'm not a piece of stone. Save your stupid games for all your other lovers." He grabbed her by the throat and pushed her onto the table. Rudy was amazed at where this sudden burst of inspiration had come from.

"Why did you do it?" Lassiter asked.

"Hchamed! Please!" croaked the slave girl, still pinned to the table.

"Don't Hchamed me!" he yelled.

The runner tiptoed over to a craft serviceman while all this was going on and handed him Annie's letter.

"This is for Rudy Valentine," he whispered. "Don't give it to him until after the audition is over."

The man nodded and the runner slipped back into the darkness.

"It's true," the slave girl said. "He told me he would ruin my father if I didn't let him play with me."

"Whore! Strumpet!" boomed Lassiter. "I want

to know the truth. Do you hear me? The truth! You filthy pig!"

"Ask! Just ask me," gasped the girl.

The craft serviceman walked quietly behind Zitz and his men, watching the commanding audition as he went. Finally, he stopped at the edge of the set, just behind Rudy, and waited for the scene to end.

"During the time when you were lying naked in his arms," Lassiter said, his eyes filled with passion and rage, "and he . . . let you have it—were you thinking of me, or were you thinking of him?"

"You," said the slave girl.

"I believe her!" Lassiter cried. "Do you hear me, God? I love this lady! And from this time on, she is as pure in my eyes as is the rain that falls from heaven."

He picked the slave girl up into his arms and kissed her passionately.

Thunderous applause followed and many flashbulbs popped. Ladies of the press beamed with delight at the actor's performance.

Zitz, also beaming, looked down to try and glean a response from the barber, who was again very noncommittal. Zitz couldn't believe it.

The craft serviceman tapped Rudy on the shoulder and handed him the letter.

"This is for you, Mr. Valentine. They told me to give it to you after the scene," he said.

Rudy recognized the writing on the envelope right away. He thanked the man, then turned away to read the letter in privacy.

> Congratulations, darling. I knew you'd win.
> I just knew it.
> I'm leaving on the noon train for Milwaukee. You don't need me here, Rudy.
> This is what you've wanted all your life. If you would just accept what you really want in your heart, we'll both be happy . . . even if we're not together. Good-bye, darling.
>
> I love you.
> Annie

Rudy looked up in a daze. The applause was just starting to die down when an assistant director called to him.

"You're on, Mr. Valentine."

Rudy stared at the man blankly.

"C'mon—you're on!"

"Rudy! Come on," shouted the director. "This is it! You're next."

Rudy slowly walked toward him, still holding Annie's letter in his hand, as the director again motioned him to hurry up.

"Annie!" shouted the director. Rudy, hearing the name, stopped short for a moment. Onto the set walked Anne Calassandro, the acting partner Rudy had nearly killed in his first audition.

"Rudy, you remember Miss Calassandro, don't you?" the director said.

They nodded to each other. Anne Calassandro

smiled, but she unconsciously rubbed her neck.

"How are you feeling today?" she asked cautiously.

"Okay, kids, get ready," the director said. Then he turned to the crowd "Ladies and gentlemen, your attention please!"

Rudy and Anne Calassandro moved into their positions as the large audience quieted down.

"May I present our third and last contestant . . . Mr. Rudy Ballantine!"

As the audience began to applaud, the assistant ran up to the director and corrected him.

"That's *Valen*tine," he said.

"Oh, Valentine, Valentine," said the director. "Excuse me, ladies and gentlemen. That's Rudy *Valen*tine! Let's have absolute quiet, everybody. Aaaaannnnd . . . " He walked over to his chair, still holding the word, " . . . aaannnd . . . *action*!"

All eyes focused on Rudy. He just stood there, still holding Annie's letter in his hand. The people of the press watched in silence. Zitz sat on the edge of his chair, eagerly awaiting some response. Nothing. He looked over at the director suspiciously.

"I said *action*, Mr. Valentine," the director yelled.

Suddenly, Rudy sparked into life. He threw away Annie's letter and walked over to Anne Calassandro.

"Hi! My name is Felix. Feel like a dance?" he said pathetically.

Anne Calassandro looked up at him questioningly, then over to the director for guidance.

"Stand up, cutie . . . let's see your stuff!" said Rudy, an inane grin on his face.

She stood.

"Oh boy, aren't you something. Whew, look at that," said Rudy, pointing to her breasts. "Woooh! You're really hot stuff. Only trouble is . . . *I don't like girls.*"

The director didn't believe what he'd just heard. He tried to avoid Zitz's cursing looks at him by burying his face in his handkerchief. The ladies of the press murmured amongst themselves and wrote the extraordinary quote down in their note pads.

"That's right. I just don't like them," Rudy said, then his voice turned into the high-pitched squeak that he used as a disguise in Valentino's tent the night before. "No sir-ee; not for me!" he squeaked.

Zitz's eyes popped. How could anybody be so rotten?

"You didn't know that, did you?" Rudy asked Anne Calassandro. "I don't like them, don't like them, *don't like them.*" He walked over to her and grabbed her by the throat. "*Do you understand what I'm saying to you? I'm saying that I don't . . . like . . .*"

Tears filled Rudy's eyes as he looked down at Anne Calassandro's breasts. The whole audience was completely stunned. He looked up at her again and a strange thing happened. Anne Calassandro became Annie, his Annie. He slowly pulled her towards him and kissed her mouth, her cheeks, her shoulders, her breasts. He dropped to his knees and kissed her waist, oblivious of the people watching him. He looked up and Annie smiled ever so slightly, calmly, lovingly.

"I love you," he said. "You're the only one I've ever loved. I just didn't know it. Can you understand that? I loved you, but I didn't know it."

Everybody continued to watch, confused.

"I love you now. I loved you when we first met. And even after you've forgotten all the pain I've caused you, and perhaps have forgotten me . . . I'll love you then. Don't leave me. Please, love me again." He buried his head into her skirt.

Zitz was stunned. He looked around him and found the women of the press weeping and sobbing. The director sobbing, the camera crew sobbing. His yes-men sobbing. He, too, despite his tough exterior, found it difficult to hold back the tears. There was a long silence. Then suddenly, a scream.

"I do! I love you!" shouted Anne Calassandro, "I love this guy!" She sank to her knees and started to kiss him all over.

Slowly, like the beginning of a heavy rainstorm, the applause started to come. Just a patter at first, but it quickly built into a torrent of thunderous applause, with whistles and yells of delight.

Zitz went crazy. He turned to the barber to see what he thought.

"That's him," he replied, grinning madly. "That's him, you big fathead!" The barber swung out with a teddy bear that was sitting on his lap and knocked Zitz backward into his yes-men. When Zitz finally struggled back onto his feet, he shouted: "That's him! That guy is The World's Greatest Lover!"

The crowd's hysteria went out of control and the women surged forward towards Rudy, with Anne Calassandro still hanging onto his neck and kissing him furiously.

The sea of ladies engulfed the astonished Rudy, ripping at his clothes, scratching and kicking each other just to get close to him. The poor director and his assistant were swamped by the ensuing crush.

"Let's clear the set, please. Ladies, come on now," he shouted. "Let's not act like children."

But it was all in vain. No one could hear him through the screams and cheers. Some of the movie crew managed to push themselves through the mob and started to pull women off Rudy.

"He's mine!" Anne Calassandro screamed. "He's mine. Please, I love him. Oh, God, I love him so much." She kicked and scratched as they dragged her away. "Hey, cut it out. I'm not foolin' around. This is for keeps. For Christ's sake, give me a break. I love him. Don't you hear what I'm saying to you? I love that man!''

Finally Rudy's head emerged from the crowd as two large men managed to lift him onto their shoulders. From this vantage point, he saw himself being pulled to safety from the frantic mob.

The two men carried the bewildered Rudy all the way across the stage and sat him on top of a handsome white Arabian horse. The crowd followed in close pursuit as Rudy and the horse were suddenly flooded with light, revealing a large oasis set.

Twenty dancing slave girls backflipped across the set and formed a pose in front of Rudy. Flashbulbs popped. People yelled and screamed as they pushed each other out of the way to get a good view of what was about to happen. Adolph Zitz sat astride a wooden horse, talking to people of the press as his yes-men pushed him towards the oasis set. A crew of men wheeled a movie camera into position right in front of Rudy. Annie's words, ''This is what you've always wanted,'' kept ringing in Rudy's ears as he watched the crowd begin to converge on him again. He suddenly spurred his horse. The Arab wrangler who had been holding the reins started to move with them as Rudy and the horse began to circle the oasis set.

''What are you doing?'' he shouted. ''Hey, Rudy! What the hell are you doing?''

Zitz, who had stopped in front of the oasis set, looked up, a little puzzled. The dancing girls turned from their pose to watch Rudy circle the water. Some photographers continued to pop photos as the wrangler pleaded with Rudy.

"Rudy, for Christ's sake, cut it out." He could just about manage to keep hold of the reins as Rudy rode faster and faster.

"Rudy!" screamed the director.

"Hey, what's happening?" yelled Zitz.

"This is what you've wanted all your life." The words echoed in Rudy's head.

He started looking for an exit. Could it be too late? Could he catch her before she got on that train? Suddenly he found an exit in the stage, but a large fake wall and a sea of press people barred his way. He grabbed a rifle from one of the soldiers and prodded the wrangler into the oasis. Then he fired a blank into the air. It echoed between the stage walls as everyone fell silent. He looked at them for a moment, then Rudy screamed at the top of his lungs:

"This is fake! This is not real life!"

He charged off towards the exit.

Zitz stood up in his stirrups and yelled to his foreign legion soldiers, "Stop that man!"

The men knelt in perfect unison and aimed their rifles at Rudy. One of them carried a sabre and issued the command: "Ready!"

Photographers and people of the press scattered as Rudy galloped towards the wall and his escape.

"Fire!" yelled the officer with the sabre, and the Legionaires showered people with clouds of smoke as their blanks exploded into the air.

Almost by instinct, Rudy's horse galloped towards the six-foot wall that separated Rudy from his freedom and, with one majestic leap, the handsome white steed carried Rudy up, up, over the wall and through the opening in the stage exit.

CHAPTER 21

THE CHICAGO EXPRESS PULLED out of Los Angeles station and quickly built up speed through the surrounding countryside.

Annie sat next to a window looking out at the approaching desert. She blew her nose one last time and put her small lace hanky back in her purse. Then she picked up a copy of *Hollywood*, a movie magazine she'd bought, and started to thumb through it. There were the pictures of the three finalists staring at her, and tears welled up in her eyes as she looked at Rudy's photo. That was the only way she would be able to see him from now on.

Her gaze drifted towards the window again at the shimmering desert and hot sun. Then suddenly a blur flashed in front of the window. She blinked the tears from her eyes and jumped back in amazement.

There was Rudy! He rode furiously on his white horse and yelled to Annie, but the train noise covered what he was saying. He started to make lewd suggestions with his eyes as he hung on desperately to the charging horse. Annie broke into laughter at the sight of him, still wearing his sheik's outfit and bouncing up and down outside her window. He managed to free one of his hands from the horse's reins for a moment and pointed towards the front of the car. She immediately jumped up and ran to the exit.

Annie opened the train door and looked back at Rudy, whose beautiful white horse was gaining on the train, pulling up even with Annie's doorway. She looked at him riding towards her and she suddenly realized that it wasn't Valentino who had swept her off her feet in all those dreams. That was just the movies. It was the hope in her heart that Rudy would be her hero. He was the dashing man on the white horse who would carry her away. She took a deep breath and jumped, landing in Rudy's arms.

"Oh boy, look at those gams," said Rudy in his high-pitched imitation Valentino voice, the one he'd used in the tent that memorable night. "What're you doin' tonight, honey? Maybe we could meet later for a little snack."

Suddenly Annie realized.

It was her husband she'd made love to in the tent. It was Rudy!

She flung her arms around his neck as the majestic Arabian reared away from the train and Annie and her sheik rode off into the desert.